"Wha　　　　　　　　　　
in the Tyson household?"

Graham's face was bleak. "Me—or the children?"

Jenny felt a tightening of her nerves. "You're implying that I see you as a means to an end?"

"Well, it fits. You can't have children. I've already got three. An ideal match. Funny—now I've found a woman willing to take on all my children and I'm complaining." Graham gave her a brotherly pat on the shoulder. But his palm brushed her smooth warm flesh. With a groan he pulled her to her feet and found her lips in a kiss of such desperation that Jenny felt the tears flood her eyes. A battle raged within her.

Tell him you love him and see what he says, urged one little voice.

Run, Jenny—or are you courting rejection? countered the other.

SANDRA FIELD, once a biology technician, now writes full-time under the pen names of Jocelyn Haley and Jan MacLean. She lives with her son in a rustic farmhouse in Canada's Maritimes, which she often uses as a setting for her books. She loves the independent life-styles she has as a writer. She's her own boss, sets her own hours, and, increasingly there are travel opportunities.

Books by Sandra Field

HARLEQUIN PRESENTS
768—A CHANGE OF HEART
799—OUT OF WEDLOCK
824—A WORLD OF DIFFERENCE
905—ONE IN A MILLION

HARLEQUIN ROMANCE
2457—THE STORMS OF SPRING
2480—SIGHT OF A STRANGER
2577—THE TIDES OF SUMMER

writing as Jan MacLean
2295—EARLY SUMMER
2348—WHITE FIRE
2547—ALL OUR TOMORROWS

writing as Jocelyn Haley
DREAM OF DARKNESS

HARLEQUIN SUPERROMANCE
88—CRY OF THE FALCON
122—SHADOWS IN THE SUN
217—A TIME TO LOVE

SANDRA
FIELD

an ideal match

Harlequin Books

TORONTO • NEW YORK • LONDON
AMSTERDAM • PARIS • SYDNEY • HAMBURG
STOCKHOLM • ATHENS • TOKYO • MILAN

Harlequin Presents first edition May 1987
ISBN 0-373-10977-6

Original hardcover edition published in 1986
by Mills & Boon Limited

CHAPTER ONE

JENNY'S first encounter with Graham Tyson was impersonal in the extreme, her second, excruciatingly personal.

Lois had phoned her the day before to invite her to Dr Tyson's lecture, which was sponsored by the History Department. 'Do come with me, Jenny. Terry's got to attend some kind of a dreary seminar in Fredericton, he'll be gone for two days, and I hate going to a lecture on my own, there's no one to discuss it with afterwards.'

'Eighteenth-century French peasantry?' Jenny said dubiously. 'Not exactly my line, Lois.'

'All the more reason why you should go—think what you'll learn. He's a fabulous lecturer, Jenny, he could talk about the composition of chicken feed and make it interesting!'

'But I was going to start organising my office tomorrow.'

'The office will keep. Graham doesn't give many public lectures, you really shouldn't miss this one. There's a gathering of all sorts of big names in the history field this week, sort of an international convention, and it's a great honour for him to have been chosen to speak.'

'Okay, okay—I give up.'

'Wonderful! I'll pick you up at seven-thirty. Good luck with the office.' And Lois had rung off.

Lois Turnbull had been a major influence in Jenny's recent hasty decision to move from New York to Brockton, a small university town in New Brunswick. Lois and Jenny had been friends for years, for Lois had been studying violin at Juilliard while Jenny studied

piano, and for two years they had shared an apartment.
Lois was one of those genuinely plain-faced women
who, because they have boundless self-confidence, a
zest for living and a flair for clothes, manage to make an
impression wherever they go. Terry Turnbull, brass-
player, had certainly been impressed. He had married
Lois the day after her graduation from Juilliard and had
whisked her off to what Lois had called 'the wilds of
Canada'. In other words, Brockton. It was Lois who had
phoned Jenny long-distance and urged her to apply for
the job in the Music Department of St Martin's
University, and Lois who had found her a house to rent
on the outskirts of the town. On the day of the lecture
Jenny had been in Brockton exactly one week.

The lecture hall was in the Arts building, one of the
gracious granite-faced buildings set among maple and
oak trees on the St Martin's campus. The university was
richly endowed and its standards were high, that much
Jenny knew; the music department was exquisitely set
in a crescent-shaped building flanked by rose bushes
and overlooking a pond on which swans floated with a
serene unconcern for the rest of the world.

The lecture hall was two-thirds full when Lois and
Jenny arrived. Delegates to the convention were
identified by name tags; the remainder of the audience
was made up of students attending summer school and
of casual visitors like Jenny herself. Lois led the way to
two seats half-way up the banked rows of chairs; she
made a striking figure in a flaming red linen shift with
batwing sleeves, her leather-thonged red sandals criss-
crossed to her knees, her crop of short black hair
gleaming under the lights. Jenny followed her, noticing
people watching their progress, knowing from past
experience that she and Lois made an interesting pair.
She was blonde where Lois was dark, her figure
curvaceous compared to Lois's almost boyish leanness,
and—she was realistic enough to recognise—her beauty

a foil to Lois's grey eyes, aquiline nose and too-wide mouth. Marc, Jenny's first fiancé, had compared Jenny to a medieval Madonna, a simile that had not pleased her in the slightest, while Samuel, her second, had likened her to Botticelli's Venus. There were times when Jenny deplored her own beauty with its ripeness and feminine allure, its contradictory hints of earth mother and ethereal goddess. She attracted men like flies. Lois, who quite blatantly wanted to marry her off, had assured Jenny that she would be introduced to every eligible male professor on campus by the time classes began in the autumn. At twenty-five, however, with two broken engagements in her past, Jenny was not at all sanguine that Mr Right was waiting for her in the wings, or indeed that he existed at all!

They settled in their seats, Lois keeping up a whispered—and occasionally scurrilous—commentary on various of their neighbours. 'There's the head of the Music Department down there, Dr Moorhead, you've met him, haven't you? The student two seats over from him is supposed to be a drug pusher, he owns a white Corvette and how else could he afford it? Three rows down to our right, do you see the blond-haired man in the blue sweater? That's Roland Petrie. He's in computer science. I'll introduce you to him, he's a bachelor, and quite handsome, don't you think? He was engaged last year and broke it off, so you'll have that much in common. Of course, you did it twice, didn't you?'

'I only broke off one of them,' Jenny muttered, very much aware that the elderly couple sitting directly below them had stopped their own conversation to listen to the more interesting one between Lois and Jenny.

Lois ignored this denial. 'I know two other men I want you to meet. One of them won't arrive until September—his name is Max Carey—but I saw the other just yesterday. Sloane Mitchell. He's a stockbroker, a teeny bit dull but well-heeled. And very good-looking.' She frowned critically at the back of Roland Petrie's unsuspecting neck. 'Better looking than Roland, I have to admit . . . oh, good, they're going to start on time.' And she settled herself in her seat, leaving Jenny, as was often the case, temporarily speechless.

Two people had entered the lecture hall by one of the lower doors and were walking towards the podium. Jenny smiled to herself as she saw the first one, because he looked exactly as a history professor should look, short, slightly stooped, with gold-rimmed glasses and a baggy tweed jacket complete with leather elbow patches. He did not look as if he would be a dynamic lecturer, but then appearances could be deceptive.

She glanced at the man following him, and blinked. Dynamic was the word for him, she thought. He did not look the slightest bit like a history professor. Who on earth was he?

She was not left long in suspense. The elderly man in the baggy tweed jacket stepped up to the podium, which was too high for him, and started to talk. 'Ladies and gentlemen,' he said, 'it is my great pleasure and privilege to introduce to you this evening Dr Graham Tyson, head of the Department of History of St Martin's University, graduate of Princeton, author of many outstanding . . .'

But Jenny heard the long list of publications and awards with only half an ear. Graham Tyson was staring studiously at the floor, hands in the pockets of his light grey suit, as if he was removing himself from his own impressive credentials. Not because he was embarrassed or ill at ease, Jenny decided, her forehead crinkling. Simply because they were irrelevant.

He was tall and rangy. His hair was dark, with a natural wave; she could not tell what colour his eyes were, although she was willing to bet they were bedroom eyes. Because if he was at ease with his accomplishments, he was also at ease with his body; she could tell that just from the way he was standing. He's the sexiest man I've ever seen, she thought blankly, and her frown deepened. He would have to be married—no one as gorgeous as he could possibly be unattached! Besides, if he were unmarried, Lois would have been threatening to introduce him.

There was a polite round of applause as the elderly man, whose identity was still a mystery to Jenny, finished his introduction and Graham Tyson strode up to the podium. He took his hands out of his pockets to clasp either side of it, and looked up at his audience. His eyes were blue, Jenny saw, a very dark blue, intense and, even at a distance of ten rows, definitely disturbing. Quite unlike the blue of Jenny's eyes, which by her various suitors over the years had been compared to cornflowers, delphiniums, and forget-me-nots.

She saw something else. Graham Tyson was not wearing a wedding ring.

When he began to talk his voice was quiet and relaxed. But as he warmed to his theme it deepened and became impassioned. He moved away from the podium; he gestured with his hands and jabbed at the air, and the French peasant of the eighteenth century rose from the dust to become a living being, up to his ankles in mud in the fields and up to his neck in a bewildering and horrifying array of tithes, rents and taxes; his wife choking over the smoke of her cooking fire, watching her children die of hunger—one less mouth to feed,one less heir among which to divide the miserable strip of land. Jenny sat mesmerised, transported to another country, another century, another culture, crossing an impossible gulf because of one man's knowledge and incredible ability with words.

When Graham Tyson finished speaking after what could have been twenty minutes or an hour, the audience paid him the compliment of a moment's utter silence. Then there was an unrestrained burst of clapping.

He looked around the crowded hall, nodding his acknowledgement of the applause. And it was then, for the first time, that his eyes met Jenny's. Among the rows of smiling faces hers stood out, still bemused, overshadowed by the tragic vision of poverty and despair that he had painted. In a moment of wordless communication, as their gazes locked, she knew instantly that he understood her bemusement and was complimented by it; she could not as easily decipher the other emotion in those dark blue eyes. Her heart was beating uncomfortably fast; her breath seemed to have caught in her throat.

Then someone asked a question, and he looked away, nor did he look back. When the questions ended a few minutes later, he was thanked by one of the history students and was then immediately surrounded by a crowd of admirers.

With single-minded purpose Lois waved at Roland Petrie, grabbed Jenny by the wrist and pulled her along to meet the young man in the blue sweater. 'Wasn't that a fabulous lecture, Roland? How are you? Roland, I'd like you to meet Jenny Sprague, who's joining the Music Department—piano. Jenny, this is Roland Petrie. Jenny and I have been friends for years, we roomed together at Juilliard.'

'Hello, Jenny, nice to meet you. What do you think of Brockton so far?'

Jenny tried to gather her wits. 'Ten days ago I was living on Forty-second Street in Manhattan, so I'm in a state of culture shock. But a pleasurable state—I grew up in Saskatchewan, so I'm used to wide open spaces. The marshes here are beautiful, aren't they?'

Brockton was surrounded by a vast area of tidal flats reclaimed from the sea; beef cattle grazed there and

weathered grey barns dotted the landscape. Jenny's
house was at the edge of the marsh, and she had
responded instantly to the windswept meadows and the
huge expanse of sky. In New York she had grown used
to seeing very little of the sky.

Roland, it transpired, had taken his Masters degree
at the University of Saskatchewan. The conversation
moved along predictably, ending with Roland promis-
ing to give Jenny a call to set up a date for dinner. Jenny
rather liked his good manners and his pleasant,
intelligent face, and she could tell that he was attracted
to her. Why, then, did she feel this ennui, an all-
encompassing boredom of the spirit, as Roland Petrie
left them at the door?

Because I'm running scared, she thought ruefully,
answering her own question. Frightened of involve-
ment, frightened of rejection. Which did not stop her
from noticing that Graham Tyson had disappeared.

Lois was jubilant. 'I knew Roland would ask you for a
date. He's nice, isn't he? I'm sure you'll find you have a
lot in common once you get to know him.'

The question was out before Jenny could stop it. 'Is
Graham Tyson married?'

Lois shot her a sharp look as they pushed open the
swing doors and emerged into the soft darkness of a July
evening. 'Oh, you don't want to get involved with him.'

'Answer the question, Lois.'

'He's a widower,' Lois said reluctantly.

She had started this; she might as well carry it to the
end. 'So is he involved with someone? Living with
someone?'

'Not with a woman, no.'

They were walking along a gravelled path beneath
huge maple trees. 'Lois, you're being perverse! He's
surely not a homosexual?'

'Goodness, no—he's the sexiest man on campus.'

'Then if he's not married, not involved, and

heterosexual, why aren't you planning to introduce me to him?'

'Darling, he's got children.'

'That's not considered a crime, you know.'

'*Three* children. Or is it four?'

'Oh.' Jenny gulped. 'His wife obviously thought he was the sexiest man on campus, too.'

'Oh, they're not all his. One, at least, was adopted. Or maybe two. It doesn't matter. The point is, no woman in her right mind wants to get involved with a man who's got three children. Or four. All under the age of eight. Now Roland's unattached and every bit as attractive——'

'Roland, as attractive as Graham Tyson? You're joking!'

'Well, nearly as attractive. And he hasn't got any children. None that I know of, at any rate. Roland is a much better prospect, Jenny, believe me . . . want to come back to my house for coffee?' Lois gave Jenny an artless smile.

'If you don't mind, I think I'll head home. I'm starting to do some work on my courses and I'm practising for the recital as well, so I want to be up bright and early in the morning.'

'You're teaching two courses, aren't you?'

'Mmm . . . pedagogy and piano literature. Plus regular lessons. It's going to be a busy fall. And as you know, I'm teaching a couple of students at the summer music camp, starting next week. The recital is at the end of it.'

'Rather you than me.' Lois gave an exaggerated shudder. 'Small children don't turn me on.'

Jenny had noticed that Lois and Terry showed no signs of producing—or wanting—little Turnbulls. As it happened, she herself might also have preferred not to work with young children. She said drily, 'The money'll come in handy. My salary doesn't begin for another month.'

'You could have stayed in New York.' There was the hint of a question in Lois's hooded eyes.

'I didn't want to stay in New York. And we are not going to discuss the reasons for that at ten-thirty at night, Lois, my love.' She gave her friend a quick hug. 'Good night. Thanks for inviting me to the lecture, I enjoyed it. See you soon.'

Lois turned right to walk to her house, only two streets away from the campus. Jenny turned left towards the car park. She drove along the quiet streets, her mind preoccupied with the friendliness of Roland Petrie, with the vagaries of Lois, who had so conclusively dismissed Graham Tyson, and last but not least with the man Lois had dismissed. A widower with three or four children. A superb speaker. A man of confidence, passion and charisma.

You don't need him, Jenny. You don't need Roland Petrie, either. You came up here to get breathing space, to get away from former fiancés and men in general. Forget Graham Tyson and his brood. He's not for you.

All of which was admirable advice, no doubt, but which did not stop her from remembering a pair of disturbingly dark blue eyes and a loose, rangy body last thing before she fell asleep and first thing when she woke up in the morning.

CHAPTER TWO

DURING the summer music camp, which was to last for two weeks, Jenny was responsible for two forty-five minute lessons each morning, at nine and ten o'clock, to be given in a practice room in the Music Department. She was given the two names that first morning: Kevin Williams and Melanie Gerritt.

Kevin arrived five minutes late. He had red hair, scuffed sneakers and a general air of being anywhere but where he wanted to be. He was not long in revealing that his parents were away for two weeks and he was attending the music camp because the basketball camp had been filled up. 'All my friends are at basketball camp,' he said. 'It's not fair.'

Life is not fair, Kevin, thought Jenny with a wry twist of her mouth. However, she set herself to draw him out and then had him play a couple of pieces. He plunked his way through a Norwegian country dance and did dreadful things to a simplified arrangement of a Bach prelude. Jenny unearthed two scores from the heap on the shelves, one a very loud, percussive piece that she thought might ease some of Kevin's understandable frustration, the other a rhythmically interesting march that sounded more difficult than it was; Kevin showed a flicker of interest and eventually the lesson ended.

Melanie Gerritt was plump and voluble, the type of child who would no doubt develop a crush on her music teacher. She pounded away on the keys with accuracy, vigour, and not a scrap of musicality. Jenny was not convinced musicality could be taught. But she was being paid to teach, so did her best.

After Melanie had gone, Jenny made herself a coffee

and went to stand by the window. A humming-bird was darting among the rose bushes, its iridescent feathers dimmed by the gorgeous hues of the petals, its movements more insect-like than bird-like. It was very beautiful. She and Marc had once stood for fifteen minutes watching a pair of humming-birds in the Botanical Gardens in Washington, in the days when love had seemed as though it would last for ever . . .

A tap came at the door. Jenny cursed her memory and called composedly, 'Come in.'

The door was pushed open and a young girl wearing pink shorts edged around it. Her hair was ash-blonde, straight and shining, while her eyes, long-lashed, were a very dark blue.

Jenny smiled at her. 'Hello. What can I do for you?'

'I . . .' the child gulped, nervously twisting her fingers, 'I want . . .'

Jenny indicated a chair by the piano and sat down in one across from it. 'My name is Jenny Sprague, I'm the new piano instructor,' she said gently.

'I know. That's why I came—because you're new.' Another frightened gulp.

The eyes fastened on Jenny's face were bright with a mixture of fear and excitement. But their colour was unmistakable. Jenny said slowly, 'Why don't you tell me your name?'

'Gillian. Gillian Tyson. Although I prefer to be called Gillie.' She pronounced the name with a soft 'g'.

So was Gillian Tyson one of the three—or four— children of Graham Tyson? Her throat suddenly dry, Jenny said, 'Can I do something for you, Gillie?'

'I want to go the music camp,' Gillie burst out. 'Will you teach me?'

Jenny frowned. 'Did you apply? I wasn't given your name.'

'No. My father doesn't want me to go. You'd have to phone him.'

'Hold on a minute, Gillie—I don't understand.'

'Dad doesn't want me taking piano lessons. But I want to *so* badly, and it's only for two weeks, you could phone him, couldn't you?'

'Why doesn't he want you taking lessons?'

'He doesn't want anyone in the family being a musician. He says there are hundreds of other things I can do. But I *want* to play the piano!'

There was no mistaking the passionate intensity in Gillie's voice. Feeling her way, Jenny asked, 'Have you ever had lessons?'

'No. But my friend Alice takes lessons, and she tells me everything she learns and lets me play her piano.'

'Then why don't you play something for me? That will give me an idea of what you can do.'

As some of the tension left the thin little body, Jenny realised that Gillie had half expected to be shown the door immediately. The child sat down at the piano stool and adjusted its height; her legs were longer and much more slender than those of the talkative Melanie. She flipped back her hair, flexed her fingers, which were also slender, and began to play.

Jenny went to stand by the window. But the humming-bird and the rose bushes were soon forgotten, obliterated by an inner excitement that grew the more she listened. The child had self-confidence and poise, a touch Melanie Gerritt would never achieve if she lived to be a hundred, a sure rhythmic sense, and most rarely of all an ability to listen to the music and draw from it everything that was there.

Gillie played three pieces. Then she dropped her hands into her lap and slowly turned her head to the window. The velvet-dark eyes were drowning in anxiety. Gillie wanted a verdict, and cared deeply what that verdict would be.

'You're a natural musician, Gillie,' Jenny said quietly, and saw the child blush with pleasure and drop her eyes to her hands. 'You should be taking lessons all the time. Couldn't you start them in September?'

The hands twisted. 'No,' Gillie whispered. 'I don't think so.'

Feeling her way, Jenny asked, 'Are you from Brockton?'

'Yes. We live just down the street.'

'Are either of your parents associated with the University?'

'My father is. He's a history professor.'

'I believe I heard him lecture last week—is his name Graham Tyson?'

'That's right. He's a very good lecturer, everybody says.'

'Indeed he is.' As head of the History Department, Graham Tyson could obviously afford piano lessons for his daughter. 'Gillie, it should be no problem then for you to have lessons next winter. Lessons are very important. You have a great deal of natural talent, but you're falling into some bad habits, I can tell that right away. I'm sure that I can help you the next two weeks, but there's no substitute for weekly lessons with a good teacher.' She would love to teach the child herself, because a talent like Gillie's was every teacher's dream.

Again Gillie avoided Jenny's eyes. 'I know I can't have regular lessons. But I thought if you spoke with Dad, I could at least come to the music camp. He might let me as it's only two weeks. 'Cause you're new here, I thought you wouldn't mind.'

It would be criminal to allow talent such as Gillie's to go undeveloped. Not giving herself time to think, Jenny said, 'Where can I reach your father?'

'He's at work. His extension is seven-one-two.'

There was a telephone on the desk in the corner. Quickly Jenny dialled the three numbers. The receiver was picked up, and a deep voice that she would have recognised anywhere said, 'Hello?'

'Dr Tyson?'

'Yes.'

'My name is Jennifer Sprague. I'm the newest member of the Music Department, and I'm teaching piano at the summer music camp. Your daughter Gillian came to see me this morning—she's here now. She wants your permission to attend the camp.'

Dead silence. Then the voice said with a dangerous lack of expression, 'Would you put her on the line, please?'

After handing Gillie the receiver, Jenny overheard two rapped questions and Gillie's monosyllabic answers. Then Gillie put down the phone. 'He's coming over,' she said, adding unnecessarily, 'he's angry.'

An angry Graham Tyson could be a formidable opponent. 'Have you ever asked him before if you could come to the camp?'

'Yes, in June. He said no.'

'I see,' said Jenny, who did not see at all. 'Why don't you play something else for me while we're waiting?'

They did not have to wait long. Graham Tyson's knock at the door was very different from Gillie's tentative tapping. Jenny said calmly, 'Please come in.'

Gillie's father was wearing tailored grey trousers and a blue shirt, and such was the force of his personality that the room seemed to shrink. Once again midnight-blue eyes fastened on Jenny's face. 'You were at the lecture,' he said abruptly.

So he remembered her. 'Yes. I very much enjoyed it.' She held out her hand. 'I'm Jennifer Sprague.'

His grip was brief but firm. 'How do you do? Now what's going on here?'

Gillie appeared to have been struck dumb. Jenny said evenly, knowing whose side she was on, 'Won't you sit down, Dr Tyson?'

But he was staring at his daughter, who met his gaze bravely, her small chin raised. 'Gillie,' he said, 'couldn't you have asked me about the camp? Why did you have to go behind my back?'

'I did ask you. You said no.'

He gave a frustrated sigh. 'But that was a long time ago. I didn't think it mattered that much to you.'

'Yes. Yes, it does! *Please* let me come to the camp, Dad! It's only for two weeks.'

He had his hands thrust in his pockets. Jenny interjected, 'For a child who has never had formal training, Gillie shows an astonishing grasp of technique and musicality.'

He glanced over at her; he looked like a man face to face with a situation that somehow violated his deepest instincts, yet who was determined to maintain his self-control. Jenny felt an unexpected surge of compassion, and to fill the silence went on, 'Gillie would have one forty-five-minute lesson with me each day, and would play in the student recital a week from Saturday. She would also take part in various group activities during the camp.'

'Please, Dad——' Gillie gasped. 'We could get Mum's piano out of storage, couldn't we? So I could practise?'

Jenny saw him flinch. 'Yes, I suppose we could.'

'You mean I *can*?' Gillie sprang to her feet.

He had capitulated more suddenly than Jenny would have expected. 'There will be conditions, Gillie—we'll discuss those when we get home. In the meantime, I'm sure we've taken up enough of Miss Sprague's time.'

'Not at all,' Jenny disclaimed. 'In fact, if Gillie is to attend the camp, I would prefer that she and I have a lesson right now.'

For a moment raw hostility blazed in his eyes. Then the rigorous self-control was re-imposed. 'Very well,' he said. His nod was curt to the point of rudeness. 'Goodbye, Miss Sprague.'

Jenny's response was a cool, ironical smile to which,

she was pleased to notice, he was not indifferent. As the door shut behind him, she said briskly, 'Let's get to work, Gillie. We've got a lot to do in the next two weeks, and we want to make the best use of our time.'

As the slender fingers relaxed in the child's lap, Jenny knew she had struck the right note. No pun intended, she thought grimly, keeping to herself her anger that a man as well-educated and intelligent as Graham Tyson could deprive a gifted child of piano lessons.

Gillie's lesson went past the allotted time, a pattern that was to continue during the entire two weeks. Gillie was a delight to work with, bright, conscientious and grateful. After two lessons 'Miss Sprague' had become 'Jenny' and the grave little smile of the first day had widened to a gamine grin, as full of charm as its owner. On the third day she volunteered the information that her mother had died nearly two years ago. 'When Jason was born. He's my brother.'

Jenny was getting the metronome out of the cupboard. She put it on top of the piano and wound it up. 'I'm sorry to hear that, Gillie. You must miss her.'

'Yes.' A tiny hesitation, then Gillie added with an adult air of defiance, 'But we manage very well.'

'I'm sure you do. Do you have other brothers and sisters?'

'One other brother, called Daniel. He's eight and I'm seven.'

So Graham Tyson had three children, not four. While Jenny was under no illusions that three children would be cheap to feed and clothe, she was equally certain that Graham Tyson's antagonism towards Gillie's love of music had nothing to do with money.

Why was he so antagonistic? Jenny did not know. Yet the antagonism was genuine: Gillie had divulged that her father was allowing her to attend the music camp only on the condition that she ask for no further lessons.

What Jenny did recognise was her inability to
abandon Gillie at the end of next week when the music
camp ended. In three days the child had made
phenomenal progress. It could not all be for nothing.
Something had to be done, she thought militantly. And
she was the one to do it.

That afternoon she called Graham Tyson's extension.
No answer. She then rang the History Department.
'May I speak to Dr Tyson, please?'

The secretary sounded both bored and uncoopera-
tive. 'Dr Tyson is taking a couple of days off.'

'When will he be back?'

'First of next week.'

Jenny said patiently 'Could you give me his home
number, please?'

'We're not allowed to give out the personal phone
numbers of the faculty.'

Jenny allowed herself a touch of sarcasm. 'Thank you
for your help,' she said. 'Goodbye.'

She reached for the phone book and flipped through
the pages until she came to Brockton, then ran her eyes
down the last page of 't's, which went from Tyndall to
Tzagarakis. No Tyson. Trust the damned man to have
an unlisted number! She added that to her list of
grievances against Gillie's father—not the least of
which was his bedroom eyes—and cheated by finding
his home number on Gillie's application form for the
music camp. However, she waited to phone him until
nine o'clock that evening, when she assumed that all his
children would be in bed. Ridiculously she found that
she was nervous. Keeping Gillie's incredible—and
neglected—musicianship in the forefront of her mind,
she dialled the seven digits. The phone was picked up
on the third ring.

'Hello?' said the voice that had wound its spell over
an entire lecture hall.

'May I speak to Graham Tyson, please?'

'Speaking.'

'This is Jenny Sprague, Dr Tyson. I'm wondering if I might see you for half an hour to discuss a matter that concerns Gillie.'

'What did you want to discuss?'

'I'd really prefer to talk to you in person.'

'Has she done something wrong?'

'By no means.' Jenny then added smoothly, 'Would you have any time free tomorrow?'

There was a brief silence. 'Very well,' he said crisply. 'Eight-thirty tomorrow evening?'

'That would be fine.'

He gave her his street address. 'It's a big grey and white house set back from the road, you can't miss it.'

'Thank you. I'll see you tomorrow.' And Jenny hung up, feeling breathless and a little afraid. Her mother would deplore the way she was poking her nose into someone else's business. Her father, a wheat farmer who had been proud of his daughter's musical abilities and who had encouraged them verbally and financially, would understand and would no doubt cheer her on. Gillie had to have piano lessons, Jenny told herself firmly. It was up to her to convince Graham Tyson of that. Very simple.

By eight o'clock the following evening it did not seem quite so simple. Jenny had practised for three hours, losing herself in the complexities of Bach's counterpoint and the brilliant disharmonies of the Ravel composition she had chosen for her recital; she had been working on it now for well over two months. Then she ate supper, showered, and tried on three different outfits before she was satisfied with her appearance. She wanted to look cool and businesslike, so she chose blue trousers of raw linen and a loosely woven top that disguised the voluptuousness of her figure. Chunky blue jewellery encircled her neck. She pulled her hair into a bun on the top of her head, but she was getting late, so instead of managing a sleek, sophisticated chignon she had to settle for wisps of hair about her ears and an untidy, if becoming, cluster of curls. After slapping on some make-up, she grabbed her keys and left the house.

The air was still, the sky gentle with the pastels of dusk. Birds twittered above the marsh. New York seemed a million miles away. Jenny got into the car, her face thoughtful, and drove into town.

She had no trouble finding the house, which was not far from the Music Department. It was a large, handsome structure with a wide porch and white-shuttered windows, its garden a tangle of shrubbery scattered with brightly coloured plastic toys. Three bicycles leaned against the side of house. A BMW was parked in the driveway.

Taking a deep breath, Jenny walked up the steps and crossed the porch, absently admiring the ornately carved woodwork on the posts. There were two doors, the outer one oak inset with bevelled glass, the inner one wide open. Jenny pressed the doorbell and waited.

No one came. She could hear voices from inside that even through the closed door sounded like a dozen children yelling at the tops of their voices. She pressed the bell again. Still no response.

While climbing the steps Jenny had been steeling herself for Graham Tyson to open the door. But no one had done so, or evinced the slightest interest in her arrival! As she stood waiting, she became aware of the same sensations that a visit to the dentist's surgery always produced: sweaty palms and a fluttering stomach. Raising her fist, she banged on the door. The shrill of voices continued unabated. She opened the door and walked inside.

The voices were a lot louder, resolving themselves into the shrieks of an indefinite number of children and the much deeper accents of a man. It sounded as if murder was being done. Jenny said loudly, 'Excuse me, please.'

She might as well have addressed the four walls. She stepped from the doorway into the hall and looked through a graciously proportioned archway at the source of all the noise.

She saw two long, bare, muscular legs, undeniably masculine, terminating in equally bare feet. The remainder of the man's body was buried under a pile of children: Gillie, pig-tailed, clad in shorts, her cheeks pink as she giggled helplessly, a tow-headed boy straddling the man's chest, bouncing up and down, and finally a very small child of undetermined sex who was lying on its belly between the man's thighs and repeating 'Dadada' in a high-pitched monotone. Squatting on one arm of the chesterfield, a pure white cat surveyed the scene with supercilious boredom.

Jenny said again, 'Excuse me, please.'

The baby turned its head and said unhelpfully, 'Dadada.' No one else noticed her presence.

She filled her lungs with air and yelled as loudly as she could, 'Will somebody please pay attention—I'm here!'

The baby stopped wailing. The cat yawned, and three heads turned in Jenny's direction. Among them was Graham Tyson's, peering around the boy still perched on his chest. 'Omigod,' said the eminent professor of history.

The boy gave a gleeful bounce. '*We're* not allowed to say that, Dad!'

'That's right, you're not,' his father agreed. He glared at Jenny. 'You're early.'

She ostentatiously consulted her watch. 'I'm five minutes late,' she said coldly, 'because I've been standing outside trying to make myself heard.'

Still flat on his back, he looked over at the very beautiful grandfather clock in the corner. 'It's seven-thirty. Didn't I say eight-thirty?'

'It's twenty-three minutes to nine,' said Jenny.

'Daniel, have you been changing the clocks again?' Graham Tyson demanded.

The boy on his chest said in an injured voice, 'Only to Toronto time, Dad. It's only an hour.'

'I told you last time not to do that again.'

'But, Dad——'

Jenny said reasonably, 'He could have changed it to Vancouver time. In which case I'd have arrived in time for supper.'

'Or to British time,' Daniel suggested. 'Then you'd have been in bed, Dad!'

Trying not to think about Graham Tyson in bed, Jenny said brightly, 'So it could have been a lot worse.'

Gillie stood up, looking rather less hoydenish than she had five minutes ago. 'Can I show you my piano while you're here?'

'Of course you may.'

Graham Tyson heaved his son off his chest, eased the baby to the floor, and got to his feet. He was very tall, and, in denim shorts and a skin-tight T-shirt with his dark hair ruffled, alarmingly attractive. His shirt had been pulled free of his waistband, exposing a strip of tanned skin to which he appeared to be oblivious and to which Jenny wished she was. She debated saying, 'It's nice to see you again,' and decided against it. *Nice* did not seem the right word. 'Good evening,' she said instead.

'Good evening,' he responded, just as politely. 'Gillie you've already met, of course. This is my son Daniel, and that's Jason on the floor.'

Jenny smiled at them, feeling oddly nervous under such a battery of eyes. Daniel's were grey, the baby's the same dark blue as Gillie's. It was after Jason's birth that Graham Tyson's wife had died . . . Jenny pulled herself together to hear Graham offer her a seat and Daniel say, 'Gillie really likes you.'

Gillie blushed. 'Shut up, Daniel!'

'You do—you said so.'

'I like her, too,' intervened Jenny, sitting in an armchair whose chintz upholstery matched that of the chesterfield. The white cat did not look like the cosy kind you took into your lap; the chair was as close to it as she wanted to get. She now noticed two other cats, a tabby fast asleep on the bookcase and a grey angora perched on the window ledge.

Jason had staggered upright. He waddled over to Jenny, leaned against her blue-trousered leg and looked up at her with a wholly beguiling smile. 'Pity,' he said.

He was beautiful, from his plump, bare toes to his mop of dark curls. Jenny felt the familiar, agonising wrench at her heart. She could never have a baby. She had known that since she was twenty, when she had had the operation that had destroyed any hope of her ever bearing children, but with the passing years the knowledge did not seem to become much easier to accept or to bear. She said, more or less steadily, unaware that Graham Tyson's eyes were fixed on her face, 'What's a pity, Jason?'

His father said in his deep voice, 'He means you're pretty.'

'Oh.' Jenny blushed to the roots of her hair. 'Oh.'

Jason held up his arms and gave Jenny another of those delicious smiles. 'Up, up, up,' he chanted.

She did not know Jason well, but she had the feeling he would continue to chant until she did as he wished. She leaned forward and picked him up, settling his sturdy little body in her lap. He reached up and grabbed at her hair. 'Pity,' he said again.

Another wheat-gold strand came free of its pins and her bun was skewed a little more off centre. 'Thank you,' Jenny said, losing herself in the midnight-blue eyes. 'You're pretty, too.'

Jason burrowed his head into her chest so that her

blouse was pulled taut across the fullness of her breasts. 'Dadada,' he mumbled, and closed his eyes.

Jenny looked up. They were all staring at her, from Graham Tyson to the white cat, their expressions ranging from irony to a yellow-eyed aloofness. Graham was the first to speak. 'Okay, you guys,' he said, 'bedtime. Grab yourselves a snack, then upstairs with you. Daniel, fix the clocks and from now on leave them on New Brunswick time, it's more convenient. Gillie, if you're going to show Miss Sprague your piano, you'd better do so now while I put Jason to bed.' He bent over to take Jason from Jenny's arms.

But like a limpet to a rock Jason was firmly attached, his chubby fists clenched in Jenny's blouse. 'No!' he protested with a forcefulness that reminded Jenny of his father. 'No, no, no!'

Jenny said gravely, 'His vocabulary is limited but effective.'

Graham knelt by the chair, the better to detach his son. Jenny could see the scattering of grey through the man's thick hair, the laughter lines around his eyes, and the cleanly sculpted mouth. Her heart was behaving most peculiarly; she felt frozen to the chair.

As Graham reached over to unfasten Jason's fingers, his hand brushed the softness of Jenny's breast. Her pulse leaped and her eyes widened so that she looked suddenly very vulnerable. Something sparked deep in the professor's eyes. He said roughly, 'You'd better stand up—I can take him from you then.'

Jenny lurched forward in the chair, but Jason was surprisingly heavy. She felt a hand at her elbow, fingers warm on her skin, and then was being levered upright. Graham took hold of Jason and pulled, Jenny freed the clutching fingers from her blouse, and Jason began to cry, a heartbroken howl.

'Don't look so worried,' Graham said. 'He always cries as if the world's coming to an end. In five minutes he'll be asleep. Will you excuse me for a few minutes, please? There are lots of books and magazines—make yourself at home.' And with Jason tucked under his arm, he left the room.

Daniel had also disappeared, carrying the white cat, leaving only Gillie standing in the middle of the worn Persian carpet. 'My piano's in the den,' she said.

The den, which also seemed to function as a library, was up three steps from the living room. It was a very masculine room, the curtains and carpets a plain, deep rust, the furniture of Scandinavian design. Books lined the walls and were heaped in the corners and on the elegant teak desk. Only the small upright piano was free of them. Needing a moment's breathing space from too many new—and disturbing—impressions in too short a time, Jenny removed a pile of books from a swivel chair and sat down. 'Play for me, Gillie,' she said. 'Please?'

Gillie was obviously delighted to comply. She sorted through the music scores on the stand and began to play a Clementi sonatina. Jenny leaned back and closed her eyes, and felt again the brush of a man's hand against her breast and the impact of a pair of midnight-blue eyes. The interview ahead of her was going to be much more difficult than she had expected, particularly as all her carefully prepared speeches seemed to have fled. She was left with a single, undeniable fact: Gillie had to have piano lessons.

Gillie played two more pieces, then started on a Beethoven *Bagatelle* that Jenny had assigned her that very day. Gillie had obviously practised it already. Jenny sat up straighter, concentrating, then got up and stood by the bench. 'You're pushing the keys too hard in that bar, Gillie. Drop your hand. Use the force of gravity—remember? And keep those fingers vertical. Try it again.'

The two of them were totally absorbed in producing the exact sonority that Jenny wanted in the chords when

Graham Tyson appeared in the doorway. He stood
there for a minute, frowning at the two blonde heads so
close together, one pale as bleached grass, the other as
richly coloured as ripe wheat in the sun. Then he said
sharply, 'It's past your bedtime, Gillie.'

Gillie hit a wrong note. Jenny winced and looked
over her shoulder. Graham Tyson had changed into a
light blue cotton shirt with the sleeves rolled up, and a
pair of dark grey cords. His hair was neatly brushed. He
did not look friendly. She said calmly, 'Sorry, we got
carried away. I'll see you tomorrow, Gillie. Sleep well.'

The child folded up her music and put it away in the
bench. Then she looked up at Jenny, her heart in her
eyes, and blurted, 'You're not coming to see Dad
because I've done something wrong, are you? Aren't I
practising enough?'

'Gillie, dear, of course I'm not!' Jenny exclaimed,
clasping the child by the shoulders. 'It's a private matter
I want to discuss with your father, so I can't tell you
about it. But believe me, you're doing extremely well
and you're a joy to teach. Now off you go to bed—and
stop worrying.'

Gillie's smile was radiant. 'Oh, that's good!' she
smiled. 'I'll see you tomorrow.' Without self-consciousness she skipped over to her father and hugged him.
'G'night, Dad.'

He bent and kissed her, love gentling his features in a
way that nearly brought tears to Jenny's eyes. She
turned away, for she had no part to play in a private
good night between father and daughter, and heard
Graham Tyson say softly, 'Sweet dreams, darling.'
Then Gillie was gone and the two adults were left alone
in the book-lined den. With none of the softness left in
his voice the man said, 'Can I get you a drink, Miss
Sprague?'

Any tendency to tears was forgotten; Jenny knew she
needed all her wits about her. 'Thank you, Dr Tyson,'

she said limpidly.

'Graham,' he said.

'Jenny,' she responded.

'I know.' He leaned casually against the door frame so that she could not have left the room had she wanted to. 'I was a little surprised that you allow Gillie to call you by your first name.'

She raised her eyebrows. 'Oh—why?'

'Gillie is only seven—not quite of an age to treat adults as equals.'

'If Gillie respects me, it is because of the way I behave with her. The way we relate. Nothing to do with whether she calls me Miss Sprague or Jenny.'

'She should show a measure of respect for your position.'

'Simply because I'm a professor of music she should respect me?' Jenny's eyes danced; suddenly she was enjoying herself. 'Come on, Graham, you know better than that. I'd be willing to bet you don't respect all your colleagues in the History Department simply because they put Ph.D. after their name.'

'I am not a seven-year-old child, Jenny Sprague.'

'A statement that demonstrates an inspired grasp of the truth!'

His smile was ironic. 'I can see I'm not going to win this one.'

She said with complete honesty, 'Gillie does respect me. Not only that, she likes me. I feel much more comfortable dealing with her on a first name basis.'

'Oh, there's no question that she likes you—we've heard a great deal about you since Monday. What would you like to drink?'

Jenny blushed and scowled simultaneously. 'Rum and Coke, please.'

'By all means. I'll be right back.' He disappeared down the steps.

The house was very quiet with all the children in bed.

Jenny had won the first round, but was under no misapprehensions that she would win the second as easily; she prowled around the den, picking up the occasional book and leafing through it, her senses alert for Graham's return. He was not long. He was carrying a tray which held a silver bowl of salted cashews, a couple of cocktail serviettes, and two tall glasses in which the ice clinked. Jenny sat down in one of the rust-coloured chairs and accepted a glass and a handful of cashews.

He sat down across from her and raised his glass. 'Cheers.'

She took a healthy mouthful. It was very good rum. She thought of Gillie, took another sip and said, 'Your daughter shows an exceptional aptitude for the piano.'

'Oh?'

Not an encouraging response. 'She learns very quickly. She doesn't just play notes, she plays with feeling, and can form her own opinion as to what the music is saying—a rare talent in one so young. She could go far.'

'You flatter her.'

'I'm telling the truth.' Jenny took another swig of the rum and ploughed on. 'Gillie told me that she wouldn't be having lessons this coming winter.'

His face closed against her. 'That is correct.'

'The reasons for that are none of my business. But Gillie's talent is. Her talent needs feeding, Graham! She needs a teacher, someone to guide and instruct and bring out the best in her—she can't do it alone. I've come here to urge you to allow her to start lessons in September. It would be criminal to let that talent go to waste!'

'That's where you're wrong, Miss Sprague.'

He was growing angry; Jenny's heart sank. She said carefully, 'Gillie told me you didn't want anyone in the family being a musician.'

'Gillie talks too much.'

'The fault was mine. She told me because I asked.'

'Then she must learn to cope with those who show far too much curiosity about matters that are not their concern.'

Jenny glared at him. 'I have already said I do not want to pry into your private affairs. But I would be evading my responsibilities as a teacher of music and as one who loves music if I were to allow Gillie's gift to pass unnoticed . . . If it is a question of money, Graham, then I would like to offer to teach Gillie next winter without charge.'

'Money has nothing to do with it.'

His words came as no surprise. 'Then perhaps we can look at it from a different angle,' she tried. 'You see, you would be doing me a favour by allowing me to teach Gillie. You must occasionally—and I know it happens only occasionally—come across students who have an insatiable urge to learn and are consequently a joy to teach. Your daughter is one of those. I would consider it a privilege to teach her.'

'I didn't think you were hard of hearing, Miss Sprague. The answer is no.'

Despite her best intentions, Jenny was also growing angry; there were patches of colour staining her cheekbones. 'You made it a condition for Gillie, didn't you? If she went to music camp—no lessons.'

'That is so.'

'Why?' she demanded. 'Why on earth would you say that?'

'I don't have to answer that question. You invite yourself to my house to make an offer which I have in no way solicited and then expect me to explain my refusal! I sincerely trust Gillie did not solicit the offer——'

'She most certainly did not!'

'Good. To get back to the point. I do not have to justify my decision to you. It stands—Gillie will not be taking lessons from you or from anyone else.'

'You're depriving your child of—of the very breath of life!' cried Jenny. 'Gillie loves music, she needs music! And she needs lessons. I'd be willing to bet *she'd* accept them.'

'She's not going to be given the opportunity either to accept or to reject them. Because I am trusting you to say nothing to her about this conversation.'

Jenny's breath hissed between her teeth. 'What do you take me for? Do you really think I'd discuss a private conversation between the two of us with your daughter?'

'I'm not at all sure what to think, Miss Sprague, But I do know this—I will not tolerate any more interference on your part, no matter how well-meaning. Is that clear?'

She had nothing to lose. 'Very clear,' Jenny said in the clipped voice of extreme anger. 'You're allowing your stubbornness, pride and insensitivity to cripple your daughter's future.'

'Kindly don't exaggerate——' he snarled.

'I'm not in the habit of exaggerating. I was sincere in my assessment of Gillie's talent and equally sincere in my desire to teach her.'

He repeated himself, his voice tight with strain. 'Neither you nor anyone else will be teaching Gillie. I do not want her focusing any part of her life around music.'

Jenny set her empty glass down on a thin-legged teak side table. 'I can't understand how a man who has made his life's work the study of history can have such a ridiculously low opinion of music—you're surely being purposely obtuse.'

'*You're* being quite exceptionally rude!'

'That's the effect you have on me,' she snapped, not bothering to deny his accusation. 'I'm not offering *you* the favour, I'm offering it to your daughter. And if you can't accept it on her behalf because you're blind to her needs, then you may be a first-rate historian but you're a lousy father!'

She had gone too far. Graham Tyson stood up. He was white about the mouth, Jenny noticed with a kind of horrified fascination, while his eyes were black with rage. 'Do you have any children, Jenny Sprague?' he spat.

She flinched. 'No. I——'

'Then you're in no position to judge what kind of a parent I am. You try bringing up three children on your own—then you can come back and I might listen to you. Until then, you can stay away. Gillie will not be having music lessons this winter.'

Slowly Jenny got to her feet. She felt sick at heart. She had not intended the interview to end this way. 'Please——' she began, scarcely knowing what she was asking.

'I'll show you to the door.'

Her anger was rekindled. There was to be no discussion, no appeal. He had spoken, and that was that. She swept past him as best she could in flat-heeled sandals and cotton trousers, flinging over her shoulder, 'I can find my own way out, thank you.'

She could hear the fall of his footsteps behind her as she crossed the living room; the other two cats were now lined up on the chesterfield. Forcing herself not to hurry, she turned at the front door and said coldly and with immense dignity, 'Good night, Dr Tyson.'

'A wonderful exit, Miss Sprague,' he said sardonically. 'You must have had practice. Good night.'

Jenny stalked down the steps, head held high, heard the door shut behind her and almost tripped on a loose board on the bottom step. Fall flat on your face, Jenny, she muttered to herself. Highly appropriate, that would be! Without a backward glance at the big grey and white house, she got in her car and drove away.

CHAPTER THREE

AT her lesson the next day Gillie betrayed no curiosity about the meeting the previous evening between her father and her music teacher, a restraint for which Jenny was grateful. She did not want to dwell on that meeting. Instead she started stretching Gillie's daily lessons to an hour and a half, trying to pack in as much as she could and to establish some solid groundwork on which, it was to be hoped, Gillie could build. She gave Gillie a lesson on Saturday morning, definitely not a requirement of the camp, and at the weekend went through the sheaves of music on her shelves at home to find suitable pieces.

She was also practising very hard for her own recital, due to take place the following Friday evening when many of the parents would have arrived; the students' recital began Saturday morning. Jenny had done a fair amount of chamber and solo work in New York, enough to know she would never be able to number herself among the top-ranked players in the world, enough also to know the hours of work required to put together a public performance. On weekdays she had been practising four hours a day, at the weekend between six and seven.

On Sunday at about four o'clock, her back, shoulders, fingers and head aching, Jenny decided to go for a run on the marshes. The week before, she had discovered a narrow dirt track that led out to the shore. Sunday had been oppressively hot, which probably accounted for her headache; it would be cool by the sea.

She changed into shorts, a tank top and her running shoes, then drove her car to the man-made ridge that

meandered along the shore, After parking the car in the
minimal shade offered by a clump of wind-beaten
spruce trees, she got out and went through her
stretching routine. The wind, which had been blowing
all day but which in town was hot and dry, out here had
the cutting edge of the distant ocean. Turning her back
on her car, she began to run along the top of the ridge.

The mud flats stretched for miles, for this was the
very head of the Fundy tidal system, source of the
world's highest tides. Marsh grass, green and pliant,
bowed to the wind; gulls wheeled overhead, their
plumage a dazzling white in the sunlight, their cries a
distillation of all the loneliness of the empty flats. Jenny
ran steadily over the parched brown earth of the ridge,
the tension leaving her body, her spirit soothed by the
sweep of sea and sky.

She went about a mile and a half, then turned around.
A bright red kite was surging up into the sky near the
gully where she had parked the car; the tail of the kite
writhed, snake-like, in the air currents. As a little girl
growing up on the outskirts of a prairie town Jenny had
often flown kites, and now she felt the long-familiar
burst of wonder and excitement as the kite soared
higher. Her feet grew wings. Her eyes were glued to the
scarlet triangle hovering in the blue sky, and as she drew
closer she saw that the tail of the kite was made up of
green and yellow streamers. She jogged along the curve
of the ridge and down the slope towards the copse of
spruce trees where she had parked the car, and as she
did so she saw for the first time the owners of the kite.
She stumbled to a halt, but it was too late. They had seen
her. 'Hi, Jenny!' Gillie yelled. 'Come and fly the kite!'

They were all there: Graham Tyson with Jason
strapped in a harness on his back, Gillie and Daniel.
Daniel was holding the kite.

Jenny covered the last few yards at a walk,
remembering how hard she had strived to look cool and

professional three evenings ago when she had visited
Graham Tyson, conscious now that she must look her
worst. She had bundled most of her hair into a pony tail,
but strands of it were clinging to the sweat on her face,
and beneath the thin tank top her breasts were heaving.
While she was not overweight, her figure was richly and
generously curved; she saw Graham Tyson's eyes flick
over her from head to foot and knew her cheeks must be
flushed from more than exertion. 'Hello,' she said. 'Isn't
it a lovely day?'

'Lovely,' Graham agreed, his gaze at the level of her
bosom, where the outline of her nipples showed through
the thin fabric.

'Dadada!' gurgled Jason, waving his arms at her.

Grateful for any diversion, Jenny said 'Hello, Jason.
Hi, Daniel and Gillie.'

'Do you run every day, Miss Sprague?' Graham
Tyson asked, with a somewhat overdone politeness.

Ah yes, she thought wickedly, we must behave in
front of the children. 'Two or three times a week.'

'A hot day for running.' And again his eyes wandered
over her sweat-dampened shirt.

'But the wind is cool up on the ridge,' she replied,
wondering inwardly which of them would take the prize
for inanity.

As if he had read her mind, he rejoined, 'A sea wind is
usually cooler than a land wind. Wouldn't you agree?'

'I would indeed,' she said demurely.

'So we have discovered something we can agree on.'

The look in her eyes was anything but demure.
Fortunately Gillie had grown impatient with the
conversation. 'Dad, can Jenny have a turn with the
kite?'

'If she wants to.'

'I'd love to,' Jenny said promptly. 'Do you mind,
Daniel?'

'The wind's pulling pretty hard,' Daniel puffed. 'Do

you think you can hold it?'

'I'm sure I can,' Jenny replied, avoiding Graham's eye. 'I used to fly kites a lot when I was a little girl.'

As she gripped both ends of the home-made wooden handle, Daniel let go, ducking under her elbow. The wind tugged at her arms and the tail of the kite snapped and crackled as if she had a live thing at the end of the rope. She followed the elegant arch of the cord into the sky, all the way to the blazingly red triangle with its writhing tail, and laughed aloud in sheer delight. She could have been eight years old again, standing on the knoll near their house with her three brothers, the kite that their father had made pulling on the rope with the same crazy lust for freedom. 'It's beautiful!' she cried, and smiled over at Gillie, who was watching her with mouth agape. 'Do you want a go, Gillie?'

Gillie grasped the handle, giving a breathless little laugh, 'It's like taking a great big dog for a walk,' she said, grinning at Jenny over her shoulder, her body braced against the wind's pull, her long blonde hair whipping behind her head like the tail of the kite.

Graham had put Jason down on the ground, where he was grubbing happily in the dirt. As Gillie and Daniel moved further down the ridge, their attention wholly on the kite, Graham took Jenny by the arm, looking her up and down in a leisurely manner before saying deliberately, 'You're quite easily the most beautiful woman I have ever met.'

Jenny's jaw dropped. 'If I'd been asked to guess what you might say to me next,' she spluttered, 'I would never have guessed that!'

'Don't you ever look in the mirror?'

She wiped her forehead with the back of her hand. 'Right now I would prefer not to!'

He stepped a little closer. The sun fell full on his face and his eyes were bluer than the sky. 'I might not have guessed that I'd say it, either.'

'Then why did you?'

'Let's call it an irresistible impulse ... I'm sure I'd find you even more beautiful were you wearing fewer clothes.'

This time she did not allow her jaw to drop. She said warmly, 'That's a line I can do without!'

'It's no line, Jenny Sprague. It's the simple truth.'

Her sense of humour, of which Samuel had never approved, got the best of her. 'The unadorned truth, you might say.'

He laughed. 'Indeed. And no, in answer to the look in your eye, I have never had a conversation quite like this in my life. Particularly with a woman whom I have only met twice and with whom I seem destined to fight like cat and dog.'

'So why me?'

'I'm—not sure. Partly, I suppose, because when I made that rather outrageous statement you neither blushed nor simpered nor slapped my face. Other than that, I don't think I can explain. I don't understand it myself.' His fingers moved on her bare arm in a feather-light caress. 'Why don't you come back to the house and join us for dinner?'

'I can't, Graham. I——'

'Heavy date?' he interrupted harshly. 'I shouldn't have asked,'

'Were I so lucky!' Jenny teased. 'Although I suppose you could say I have a heavy date, yes—with the grand piano. Three more hours' practice at least.' At the blank look on his face, she added patiently, 'I'm giving a recital next Friday—hasn't Gillie mentioned it?'

He dropped her elbow, his face tight with anger. 'So the piano rules your life.'

'No, it doesn't!' she retorted. 'But the recital's important to me and I want to do well. And to do well, I have to practise—why are you so angry?'

'It doesn't matter.'

'That's a downright lie!'

'You certainly believe in speaking your mind.'

'Yes.' She frowned at him. 'You'd prefer I was turning down your invitation because of another man, wouldn't you? Rather than for the piano.'

'Almost, yes.'

'I really don't understand this—this *phobia* you have for a wooden box equipped with some bits of metal and felt and a set of ivory keys!'

'There's no reason why you should.'

Her eyes challenged him. 'So is Gillie allowed to go to the recital?'

'She's insisting I go with her.'

'Brave girl. In that case I'd definitely better go home and practise.'

Jenny stepped back a couple of paces, wondering how the cold-eyed man in front of her could be the same one who had called her beautiful. That he was drawn to her and repulsed by her simultaneously was obvious, a phenomenon that was as mysterious as it was unsettling. Quickly, before she could say anything else, she called goodbye to Gillie and Daniel.

Graham Tyson did not say goodbye; he simply stood there, watching her, his expression inscrutable. Jenny drove home, turned on the tape recorder, sat down at the piano and blanked her mind of everything but Beethoven's Sonata in F minor.

The days passed; the recital, inexorably and inevitably, came closer. Jenny worked hard at the music camp, practised her recital pieces and tried to ignore her growing nervousness. Early on Tuesday evening she had supper with Roland Petrie, then went canoeing with him on a lake just outside of town; when he dropped her off at her house so she could put in another couple of hours at the piano he kissed her on the mouth, an experience that was as pleasant as he was himself, but which inspired her to no new pianistic feats. On Wednesday she went for a run by the shore, which was deserted, and thought about a blue-eyed man and his passel of children. On Thursday afternoon she went to the hall where the concert was to be held, and went through her entire programme from beginning to end, Without vanity, she was pleased with the results; with a tightening of her nerves she wondered if she could do as well the following evening. She drove home, read an Amanda Cross mystery, went to bed and slept well.

Her pupils took up the morning. While she had managed to capture enough of red-haired Kevin's interest to produce a noticeable improvement over two weeks, Melanie Gerritt played as complacently and unfeelingly as she had done the very first day. Certainly she had learned four new pieces—but that was all she had learned. Gillie, of course, had made tremendous strides, but since Friday was to be the child's last lesson for many months Jenny did not think that much cause for congratulation.

Gillie thought otherwise. As she got up to leave at the end of the lesson she said, a catch in her voice, 'I've loved every minute of our lessons Jenny—thank you.'

'I've only scratched the surface,' Jenny replied honestly. 'But you've been a wonderful student.'

'I'll miss you.'

'I'm sure we'll see each other occasionally.'

'I asked Dad if I couldn't have lessons from you over the winter, but he said no. He didn't like me asking,' Gillie added with the frankness of the very young. 'Would you mind if I sometimes called you on the phone, Jenny, or if we went for a walk sometimes and just talked about music?'

'I'd love that. And I'll see you tonight and again tomorrow.'

'I'm wearing my good dress to your recital. Mrs Layton is ironing it for me.' Mrs Layton was the housekeeper. 'And Dad's wearing a suit. He said he'd better look his best because he was my escort. Escort is a nice word, isn't it? I'm glad it's just the two of us coming to the recital, not Daniel as well. That doesn't happen very often.'

'There's a reception after the recital—you be sure your father brings you to that, won't you? I must go, Gillie—see you tonight.'

Jenny ate a light lunch at the university cafeteria, then decided to get the mail while she was in town; she would practise for a couple of hours when she went home. Anything to pass the time, she thought, wishing her nerves didn't feel quite so much like piano wire stretched beyond its level of tolerance.

The post office was very busy. Among the collection of magazines and circulars stuffed in her mail box was a letter from her father. He had watched her suffer through pre-concert nerves before; she would be willing to bet he had planned for this letter to arrive the day of her recital.

She tore open the envelope, took out the two sheets of closely written paper and ran down the steps. Her mind more on the first paragraph than on where she was going, Jenny turned round the corner of the building and collided head-on with someone going the opposite way. The bundle of magazines fell to the ground and the breath was knocked from her body.

She looked up into midnight-blue eyes tinged with amusement and with another emotion considerably more primitive than amusement, and became aware of strong arms around her body, of her palms flat against the man's chest, of the heavy beat of his heart and the warmth of his skin. She remembered Gillie, who had had her last lesson that morning. The overstretched wire snapped. 'Can't you look where you're going!' she flared.

Graham Tyson stepped back a pace, bent and picked

up the scattered magazines. Straightening, his movements without hurry, he passed them to her. 'My dear Miss Sprague,' he drawled, 'your beauty blinded me!'

'Don't you "dear Miss Sprague" me! If Jenny's good enough for your daughter and for the rest of the world, it's good enough for you. I don't think I've ever met a man as damnably attractive as you whom I've disliked as much as I dislike you!'

He put his head to one side. 'You know, the first time I met you I wondered why on earth you weren't married—because if I'm damnably attractive, you're stunningly beautiful. However, upon closer acquaintance I'm beginning to understand. You have the insensitivity of an alligator and the temper of a shrew.'

He made his statement in a pleasant, even voice, which in no way detracted from its impact. So her visit to plead Gillie's case had been construed as insensitivity; and her personality was such that in his opinion no sensible man would marry her! Jenny said nastily, 'Since we're into comparisons, your personality is as poisonous as a snake's and as vicious as—as a shark's.'

'Sharks aren't necessarily vicious. They kill only to eat,' he said mildly.

'There must be some creature in the animal kingdom that enjoys the infliction of pain,' she retorted.

'So there is ... the two-legged one called *Homo sapiens*.'

The glint in his eye was impossible to resist. 'Which brings me back to you as a prime example, and to hell with the fancy similes. Graham, I'm sorry I lost my temper. I've got a flourishing case of pre-recital nerves—but I didn't have to take them out on you.'

His voice was flat. 'So, if recitals are hard work and agony on the nerves, why do you give them, Jenny?'

'I'm a masochist,' she said fliply.

'I asked you a serious question.'

She met his eyes, saw they were indeed serious, and

was ashamed of her reply. Choosing her words with care, she said, 'Because I love music. I want to give the audience, to the best of my ability, the experience of that music so they too might love it. I see that as my responsibility, one that unfortunately I can't shirk simply because of the work and the mental turmoil it causes me.' She grimaced, 'End of sermon.'

Briefly he took her hand in his, spreading the slim, capable fingers with their short nails, and staring at them as if they could answer a question he had not even formulated. Then he looked up. 'Come on, I'll buy you a coffee.'

'But I——'

'If nothing else, it'll pass the time.'

'I've always hated that phrase.'

'But it would apply to the day of a recital.'

She sighed, wriggling her shoulders. 'If only I could go to sleep and wake up at ten o'clock this evening with everyone madly clapping a bravura performance!' Her smile was self-deprecating. 'It doesn't work that way, does it? A coffee would be lovely, then I must get home and practise for a couple of hours.'

Across the street from the post office there was a little coffee house, which served capuccino, espresso, and herb teas, along with luscious and fattening desserts. In deference to the recital Jenny ordered plain tea. Then, suddenly shy, she said, 'I enjoyed flying the kite on Sunday ... tell me about your children, Graham. Daniel is the eldest, isn't he?'

'Yes, Daniel's eight. He's my cousin Tom's child. Tom and Marie were killed in a plane crash five years ago, so Mona and I adopted him. Gillie's seven—she's mine. Jason also is mine. My wife died after Jason's birth.'

'I'm sorry.' What else was there to say?

His face gave nothing away. 'We manage,' he said. Gillie had said the same thing. You're lucky, Jenny wanted to cry. You have a family, children of your own to love and cherish. You're a rich man, Graham Tyson—richer than I'll ever be. She said none of this. Gulping down her tea, she remarked, 'Gillie informs me that as her escort you are wearing a suit tonight.'

His smile did not quite reach his eyes, 'Gillie's looking forward to the recital tremendously.'

She hesitated. 'But you're not.'

Absently he played with his spoon. 'If I had my way, I wouldn't come anywhere near your recital tonight.'

Aware of a hurt that was far too acute, Jenny said stiffly, 'I hope you haven't told Gillie that,'

'No. Nor will I.' He glanced up. 'Jenny, don't look like that! It's just—oh hell, I can't explain.'

'Can't or won't?' She drained her cup. 'I've got to go. Thank you for the tea.'

Graham took her by the wrist. 'I know I'm not making any sense to you. But good luck tonight, Jenny.'

She sensed the words were an immense effort. 'Thank you,' she said gravely. 'Goodbye, Graham.' Then she left the café.

All the way home she thought about him. Being with him was like sailing in unknown waters without chart or compass, she decided: no signals to warn one of reefs, no markers to keep one from the strong, surging currents. She seemed destined to dash herself against those reefs, and if she were not careful, she could drown in the currents.

At half past seven Jenny entered the music building by one of the side doors, having no desire to meet anyone she knew, and went straight to the artists' room whence she would go on stage.

It was a comfortable enough room, with deep armchairs and a pretty dove-grey carpet; a grateful alumnus had donated an oil painting of the rose garden outside. Jenny prowled up and down, her grey-blue chiffon skirts swishing, her face abstracted. 'There are no heroes in the moment before a recital.' She did not know who had said that, but as far as she was concerned it was totally, woefully true.

One of the students who was acting as an usher informed her of the time five minutes before the recital was due to start; the hall was apparently three-quarters full. The same student came at three minutes after eight to tell her the lights had dimmed.

Jenny took two long, slow breaths, moved her head and shoulders to ease the tension, and flexed her fingers. She sent a succinct, but heartfelt, prayer heavenwards. Then, her face set, she pushed open the door and walked on stage.

The lights were very bright, the faces of the audience, who had started to clap when she appeared, a merciful blur in which she could not possibly have distinguished individuals. She bowed in acknowledgement of the applause, sat at the bench and adjusted it slightly. Then, hands in her lap, she gazed at the keyboard and heard the first chords of the Bach prelude sound in her brain. Raising her hands, she began to play.

Within a minute or two her nervousness had vanished. She was alone with the music for which she was responsible, the music that she loved . . .

The applause after the Bach, the three Nocturnes by Chopin and Ravel's *Gaspard de la Nuit* passed over her like a dream; she spent the intermission in the artists' room thinking her way into the Beethoven *Apassionata* Sonata. Again she walked out on the stage to applause, this time far louder than the initial polite response to an unknown quality. And again she waited until the first notes were sounding in her head before she started to play.

As the last notes died away and she lifted her hands from the keyboard to let them rest in her lap, the applause was thunderous. Numbly Jenny stood up, letting it wash over her in waves. She made three curtain calls, played Prokofiev for an encore, bowed again and went back to the artists' room. She had played better than she had ever played in her life before. And she was exhausted, physically, mentally, and emotionally.

The recital was over. She must attend the reception and then she could go home.

Still feeling as though she was in a dream, Jenny touched up her lipstick and left the artists' room, to be immediately engulfed by members of the audience, most of whom she did not know, and by a sea of congratulations and compliments. Roland Petrie kissed her warmly on the cheek; Lois hugged her fiercely and told her she was wonderful; the head of the Music Department, Dr Moorhead, called for silence and made a pompous little speech of appreciation and welcome to the 'new and very charming member of the Faculty of Music,' during which Jenny tried hard to look suitably modest and appreciative. She used the opportunity to glance around for Gillie.

Gillie and her father were standing together at the fringe of the crowd. Graham Tyson looked indecently handsome in his suit, while even across the width of the room Jenny could tell that Gillie was incandescent with excitement. As soon as she could she escaped from Dr Moorhead's pink-cheeked gallantry and elegantly rounded phrases, and made her way across the room. 'Hi, Gillie,' she said. 'Hello, Graham.'

Gillie's eyes were huge. 'You were wonderful,' she said solemnly. 'I loved everything you played.'

Jenny knelt in a swirl of chiffon, to bring her eyes to the child's level. 'Thank you, Gillie. That's the nicest thing you could have said.'

'Will I be able to do that some day?'

Graham Tyson's hand was also at Jenny's eye level. She saw the fingers curl in upon themselves, the skin pulled tight over the tanned knuckles. She said with complete honesty and with all the generosity of her nature, 'You will be able to play far better than I, Gillie. I mean that.'

Graham's nails were digging into his palm. Gillie said breathlessly, 'Me? *Really?*'

'Yes, really . . . your dress is very pretty, by the way.'

'Thank you,' Gillie gasped. 'This has been the best evening of my whole life!'

Slowly Jenny straightened, and her gaze met Graham's in deliberate, unspoken challenge. Give the child lessons, her brilliant blue eyes said.

Mind your own business, his taut face replied.

Sweetly, as if the little interchange had never happened, Jenny said, 'And did you enjoy the recital, Graham? I hope it was worthwhile putting on your suit.'

His eyes were cold. 'You'll never make it to Carnegie Hall.'

Jenny drew a sharp breath, for after so many congratulatory remarks his criticism seemed all the more scathing. 'I have no ambitions to be in Carnegie Hall.'

'Come off it. Every musician wants to make it to Carnegie Hall. You know damn well you'd rather the applause tonight had come from a more sophisticated audience—a New York audience, accustomed to the top artists of the world.'

Determined not to show how he had hurt her, she said, 'Four years ago I came to terms with the fact that I do not have the talent or the drive to make it to places like Carnegie Hall.'

'I don't believe you,' he said scornfully.

Jenny had had a long and trying day. She gripped the stem of her wine glass, thinking how much pleasure it would give her to dash its contents into his face.

His eyes sardonic, Graham drawled, 'Don't do it, Miss Sprague. Although I do admit that stuff's not fit to drink—Canadian wine at its undoubted and unparalleled worst.'

'I wouldn't waste a better quality wine.'

He had the audacity to laugh. 'One thing about you—you're rarely stuck for an answer! What are you doing when all this is over?'

'Going home to get drunk, I should think.'

'I have an alternative plan—come back to the house with Gillie and me. I'll make you a rum and Coke that will pack more of a punch than that wine.'

Jenny did not want to go home to the empty house and the inevitable slump that followed a recital. 'I accept,' she said recklessly. 'On the condition that we don't talk about anything to do with the piano.'

'Done.'

A grey-haired woman in a flounced burgundy dress unsuited to her age or her weight was bearing down on them with an air of determination. 'Excuse me,' said Jenny, and tried to collect her wits; Lois had introduced her to the woman in the grocery store last week, but the name had completely slipped her mind. She plastered a smile on her face and hoped for the best.

The reception lasted another fifteen or twenty minutes. Then Jenny gathered up her bag and her shawl and left with Graham and Gillie. They walked from the music building to his house, which although only a short distance was quite long enough for Jenny to wonder why she was being so foolish as to spend more time with Graham Tyson. The man was dynamite, Dangerous. Unpredictable. The last thing she needed . . . particularly right now, when within two hours her mood had swung from pre-recital terror to post-recital exhilaration. A recital did not leave one feeling sensible and cool-headed. One rum and Coke and then I'll go home, she thought. One can't do any harm, can it?

Once they arrived at the grey and white house, the babysitter was despatched home and Gillie despatched to bed. 'Good night, Jenny,' the little girl said.

Impulsively Jenny bent and kissed the child's cheek. 'Good night, dear,' she said. 'Tomorrow it's your turn to play in a recital.'

'Everybody's coming except Jason. I hope I'll do okay.'

'You'll play to the very best of your ability because that's the kind of musician you are. I'll see you there— sleep well.'

Gillie left the room. As soon as she was out of sight, Graham said roughly, 'She worships you.'

Jenny said provocatively, 'Get her another music teacher—she'll soon forget me.'

'I can't and she won't.'

'Jealous?' she murmured.

He stepped closer, his feet soundless on the living room carpet. 'Not as far as Gillie's concerned. But Roland Petrie's not your type.'

She should have made a crushing retort. Unable to think of one, she queried weakly, 'Roland?'

'All my children are very taken with you. Daniel saw fit to tell me he'd seen you out with Roland one evening. Then I saw him kiss you tonight.'

'Quite a spy system you have!'

'Isn't it? You have to realise that Brockton is not New York. Everyone in Brockton is intensely interested in everyone else's doings, Undoubtedly more is known about your relationship with Roland than you know yourself.'

'I do not have a relationship, as you so politely put it, with Roland. And if I did, I wouldn't discuss it with you.'

'He's a nice enough guy. But there's no music in his soul, Jenny—he's not for you.'

'And what about Sloane Mitchell? Or haven't your spies caught up with him yet?' Lois had introduced her to Sloane the same day she had introduced her to the woman in the burgundy dress.

'Sloane? Good God—he'd bore you to tears.'

On the basis of a ten-minute conversation with Sloane Jenny had already come to the same conclusion. 'Do you run a column in the newspaper, Dr. Tyson? Advice to the lovelorn?'

'Maybe I should. Because I'm right about both of them, aren't I, Jenny?'

'You are, of course,' she said agreeably.

He took another step closer and said softly, 'So have my spies missed anyone else, Jenny? Or have I managed to demolish your social life?'

'You have indeed. The men of Brockton are not exactly beating a path to my door.'

'And is there no one waiting for you back in New York?'

Her lashes flickered, 'No. Very definitely not.' Marc had married someone else; Samuel was transferring to the Chicago Symphony in september.

'There was someone.'

'*Was* is the operative word.' Two of them, not one. But there was no need to share that with him.

He said soberly, 'I'm sorry, Jenny. Because you've been hurt, haven't you?'

'You're much too perceptive, Graham Tyson.'

'Some day you'll tell me about him.'

'I thought I was to be given a large rum and Coke.'

'You will tell me, Jenny.'

'We'll see about that. Where's my drink?'

'I'll get it in a minute. I have something else in mind first.'

'Nothing you could have in mind would match the salutary effect of a very tall rum and Coke with lots of rum and not much Coke.'

'Oh? We'll see about that, too.' And he took a third step towards her, enfolded her in his arms and kissed her.

It was a comprehensive and lengthy kiss, a devastating combination of generosity, subtlety, and passion. Because his mouth was on hers, Jenny could not have talked had she wanted to, but she was struck dumb to her very soul. In the unlikely surroundings of an auditorium during a lecture on French peasantry she had recognised Graham Tyson to be a man of intense emotion; had she needed any confirmation of that conclusion, she now had it. Regrettably, he called up in her a level of emotion every bit as intense as his. She could have called it lust ... but she knew better.

Eventually his mouth left hers and he stepped back, dropping his arms to his sides. 'I've been wanting to do that for quite some time,' he said.

Her heart was racing much as it had been five minutes before the recital, although for very different reasons; she felt all the exultation of those last crashing chords of the *Apassionata*. She said faintly, 'Do you have to look so pleased with yourself?'

'Indeed I do. You look rather delighted with the world yourself, Jenny Sprague.'

'Certainly the rum has become superfluous.'

'I think we should do it again.'

The second kiss was more intoxicating than the first, even though Graham kept his hands firmly at her waist and her body a distance from his own, allowing only his mouth to speak to her of his desire. Jenny was trembling when it was over. She said shakily, 'This is ridiculous. You don't even like me.'

'I never said that.'

'You don't like my profession.'

'That's closer to the truth ... although I'm sorry I made that remark about Carnegie Hall, Jenny—it wasn't called for.' He ran his fingers through his hair. 'You played beautifully. If I may misquote one of the Greek poets, with your own two hands you touched the sky.'

None of the compliments she had received that evening had pleased her as this one did, perhaps because Graham was being totally honest despite an inner conflict whose source was still a mystery to her. She felt the prick of tears and blinked them back. 'Thank you,' she quavered.

'You shared with me your love of music, and I am the richer for it.'

'Then why do you dislike my profession so much? Graham, *won't* you let Gillie take lessons?'

'No, Jenny. Don't start that again.'

'I told the truth tonight,' she said unflinchingly. 'Gillie could indeed be better than I will ever be.'

'No.'

The mood of accord between them, of unspoken excitement and sexual tension, was gone. Jenny said humourlessly, 'You're going to save your rum—because I'm going home without it ... Graham, I don't understand.'

'Even if you did, it wouldn't make any difference.'

Voice and features were inflexible, as unyielding as granite. 'You're a hard man, Graham Tyson,' she said slowly. 'Tell me something—how old are you?'

'Thirty-four.'

'Old enough to have learned that while there are times for rigid principles, there are equally times for compromise,'

'This is not one of them.'

'Then there's nothing more to say.' She turned to leave. 'Good night.'

'I'll walk you to your car.'

'There's no need for that.' She allowed herself a touch of malice. 'As you said earlier, this is Brockton, not New York.'

'Jenny, I——'

She waited, hope flaring in her breast. But then he said in a deadened voice. 'Good night, Jenny.'

Not trusting herself to speak, she let herself out and walked down the steps, holding up her long skirts, wondering if any of the neighbours were watching. If so, their curiosity would no doubt be exercised by the brevity of her stay. He's as stubborn as a mule, she addressed them silently—and unoriginally—as she tapped along the pavement. As immovable as an elephant. As deaf to reason as an ox. And . . . dammit . . . as glorious as a wild stallion and as dangerous as a panther.

Her stock of adjectives and animals appeared to be depleted. Jenny crossed the street to the car, unlocked it and drove home. In a thoroughly bad mood she went to bed.

CHAPTER FOUR

BROCKTON drowsed under the August sun. According to the residents of the town, it was an exceptionally hot summer. Jenny, used to New York summers, found the weather blissfully cool and fresh, the wind from the marshes laden with the scent of mown hay and wild roses. She did a lot of the reading for her courses on the back porch where she could listen to the birds twitter back and forth. She watered the flower gardens and raked the lawn. She played the piano.

Sloane Mitchell invited her for dinner at a local inn renowned for its cuisine. Although his entire conversation revolved around matters financial, he was scandalised by Jenny's assumption that she would contribute to the bill; he might be rich but he had very little sense of humour. The next time he called, Jenny had plans to go shopping in St. John with Lois, and the third time she produced a fictitious excuse. He did not call again, which suited her fine. She did see Roland occasionally. Although he had divulged the long and complicated saga of his broken engagement to her on-the-whole sympathetic ear, she did not share with him the story of either Marc or Samuel. There was no reason to: she would never be intimate in any sense of the word with Roland. If she ever doubted that supposition, she had only to remember Graham's devastating kisses. *Those* had been intimate.

She had talked to Graham briefly at the music camp recital, the day after her own recital. Gillie had been the star of the show, a fact Graham was certainly astute enough to recognise. He and Jenny had exchanged a few stiff words when it was all over, and she had not seen him since.

Gillie had phoned twice, ostensibly with technical questions about the Beethoven and Bach pieces she was practising, although Jenny soon decided it was more to talk in a general way about music—a realisation that kept the fires of anger burning within her towards the child's father. She did not phone Gillie herself for the obvious reason that she was afraid Graham Tyson would answer the phone, nor did she actively encourage Gillie to phone her; but she did not discourage her, either. Gillie, ever if only seven years old, had a right to choose her own friends. Jenny was aware that this assumption could lead to trouble, and so it did. But first occurred the incident of the cat.

Jenny was walking down the front steps of the Music building one warm afternoon in mid-August, her arms laden with books from the library, when a red car rounded the corner by the church in a squeal of tyres and gunned past the Music Department, the blaze of punk rock from its stereo system almost as loud as the souped-up roar of its motor. Jenny glared after it. She had no patience with that type of exhibitionism.

As she reached the wrought iron gate that led on to the pavement, she glanced down the street. The red car was racing towards Gillie's house. As if it were all happening in slow motion, she saw a white cat emerge from the bushes and streak across the street towards the house. The driver of the red car slammed on his brakes; Jenny saw the rear of the car swerve and heard the scream of rubber on macadam. Then the red car straightened and gathered speed again.

There was a white patch on the road, a patch that did not move. Jenny began to run.

Her arms were aching from the weight of the books and her feet were hurting in their narrow-fitting sandals by the time she reached the driveway of Graham's house. She scarcely noticed. Dumping the books on the grass, she ran out on the road.

The cat was dead. Feeling sick, she stared down at it, aware of a fierce anger against those who carelessly strike down living creatures and do not even bother stopping to see what they have done. She had recognised the cat immediately—it was the white one that had sat on the chesterfield on the occasion of her first visit to the Tyson house.

Behind her the front door banged and she heard someone run down the front steps. 'Where's Snowflake?' Daniel cried. 'Did the car hurt him?'

Jenny shielded the cat's body with her own and turned her head. 'Daniel, I want you to go in the house and fetch me a box,' she said authoritatively. 'Right now.'

Daniel stopped by the gate. 'Why? Where's Snowflake?'

More gently she said, 'He was hit by the car, Daniel. I'm afraid he's dead.' She saw the grey eyes flood with tears as the boy took an instinctive step forward. 'I don't want Gillie to see him. You find me a box and I'll put him in it.'

'Are you sure he's dead?' Daniel quavered.

In her mind's eye she saw the crushed rib cage and the scarlet blood that had soaked into the white fur. 'Yes, I'm sure. I'm so sorry, Daniel—but he couldn't even have realised what hit him.'

'He didn't even stop!' Daniel burst out, and he was not referring to the cat.

'No. People can be very cruel. Go and get the box—okay?'

Daniel scrubbed at his eyes; his nose was pink. 'Okay.'

Jenny stayed where she was. The occasional car drove past, and she waved on those who would have stopped. She didn't know if she was doing the right

thing in protecting the children from the sight of the
dead cat; possibly the psychologists would say death is
part of life and therefore should not be avoided. But she
did not want to expose them to all the ugly little details.

Daniel came back carrying a box which, ironically,
had held a dozen cans of cat food, but which was sturdy
enough and large enough to hold Snowflake. 'Thank
you,' Jenny said. 'You go back in the house now,
Daniel—don't let Gillie come out. I'll be there as quick
as I can. Off you go.'

You sound as though you've been raising children all
your life, Jenny, she told herself. Then she steeled
herself for the task ahead.

Fortunately it did not take long. She managed to
arrange the cat in the box so that only his head,
untouched by the car, showed. She shut the gaping jaws,
but could not face trying to close the wide, yellow eyes.
Then she picked up the box and headed for the house.

Daniel was hovering at the door. Gillie, very pale and
composed, was standing by the archway. Jenny stepped
into the hall. Now what? she wondered, regarding the
two miserable faces in dismay.

Instinctively she repeated what she had already said
to Daniel. 'I'm sorry Snowflake's dead, Gillie. But he
died instantly, he wouldn't even have seen the car . . .
would you like to see him?' She put the box on the floor
and opened the lid.

She had done the right thing. As Daniel and Gillie
peered down at the cat, Jenny put an arm around each
of them. Then a woman in a white uniform walked out
of the kitchen.

Jenny looked up. 'Hello,' she said politely. 'You must
be Mrs Layton. I'm Jenny Sprague, a friend of Gillie's.'
It would surely be stretching the truth to say she was a
friend of Graham's.

Mrs Layton had suspiciously dark hair arranged in
tight little curls, like the stylised waves in old Japanese

prints. But her smile was friendly. 'What's in the box?' she asked, wiping her hands on her apron.

Gillie cried, 'It's Snowflake. He got hit by a car!'

'Oh, dear me ... that's an awful shame, now. I'm right glad you're here, Miss Sprague. I faint at the very sight of blood.' And the ingenuous brown eyes rolled up in their sockets.

Gillie reached down and stroked Snowflake's cheek. 'Poor Snowflake,' she crooned. 'He's not even breathing. Is that why he's dead?'

The medical ramifications of this question were beyond Jenny. 'Yes,' she said.

'We should bury him,' said Daniel.

'In the garden,' Gillie supplied.

'We could have a proper funeral,' Daniel went on.

'There's stones we could put on the grave, like in a real cemetery,' said Gillie. 'And flowers.'

Daniel took over. 'I'll get the shovel out of the shed. Where'll we put him?'

'Under the beech tree,' Gillie said decisively.

'So long as there's not too many roots. Come on, Jenny, you bring Snowflake. You can be the minister.'

'Will your father mind if you dig a big hole in the garden?' Jenny murmured.

'Oh, no,' Gillie said. 'He only minds if we disturb all the stuff in his office.'

'That makes him very angry,' said Daniel in the hushed tones of one remembering a specific incident.

'There'll be a nice chocolate cake ready when you come in,' said Mrs Layton, who obviously wanted to make a contribution to the funeral as long as it did not involve the dead cat. 'But you be sure and wipe your feet at the back porch if you've been digging.'

'I'll see they don't make a mess,' Jenny promised, and picked up the box, now promoted to a coffin, from the floor.

The back garden was a child's delight, with an oak

tree complete with home-made tree house, a tangle of
bushes perfect for playing hide-and-seek, a set of
swings, and gardens in which black-eyed-susans and fat
orange marigolds bloomed untrammelled. Daniel began
digging a hole under the beech tree, where the ground
was so shaded that very little grass grew. Gillie, who still
had not shed a tear, stayed by Jenny's side, one small,
cold hand tucked into the warmth of Jenny's. 'I'm glad
you're here,' she said, then lapsed into silence, absorbed
in the preparations for the cat's burial.

As the hole got deeper, Jenny did a share of the
digging while Gillie went to look for rocks and to gather
flowers. The digging was hard work; Jenny was grateful
for the shade of the shiny, rustling beech leaves.
Eventually Daniel said, 'I think that's deep enough,
don't you, Jenny?'

The unfortunate Snowflake would be at least two feet
underground. 'I think so,' Jenny panted. She rested the
shovel against the tree and brushed her palms against
her skirt. Then, knowing she was the one to do this, she
knelt down and lowered the box into the hole.

'We should say a prayer like in a real funeral,' said
Daniel.

Slowly Jenny stood up. Both children were eyeing her
expectantly. She swallowed, her brain working frantically, knowing that in her many hours of teaching she
had never been faced with a dilemma quite like this.
She hesitated, then with due solemnity said, 'Let us
pray.' The children bowed their heads.

Jenny swallowed again. 'We commend the soul of
Snowflake the cat to Your care,' she pronounced.
'Please comfort all those who mourn his passing.
Amen.'

Daniel picked up the spade and began to fill in the
hole. 'Isn't there something about ashes and dirt?' he
puffed.

'Ashes to ashes and dust to dust,' Jenny said. Daniel,

she realised with a wrench of pity, had lost his parents and his adoptive mother in the past five years, and could be expected to know about funerals. But the boy's face was so intent upon his task that she felt a sudden, strong rush of affection for him. Daniel coped with grief by immersing himself in the practical; there were worse ways.

When the earth was tidily smoothed over, Gillie outlined the grave in little stones and stuck flowers in the soil. Daniel leaned on the shovel and watched.

'There,' Gillie said finally, sitting back on her heels. 'That looks pretty. Jenny, has he gone to Heaven?'

'Yes,' Jenny answered firmly, trusting that she was not hopelessly corrupting their theological training.

'Cat Heaven or people Heaven?'

'I don't really know, although I'd like to think that they're the same.'

'Me, too.'

With evident interest Daniel asked, 'Where do *you* think Heaven is, Jenny? I had an argument with my Sunday school teacher because he said it was within us, which is silly, I think. I bet Snowflake's up in a tree somewhere that's full of birds.'

Dogma had never been Jenny's strong point. 'If you remember Snowflake with love,' she said carefully, well aware that she was getting into doctrinally deep waters, 'then he is within you.' She added, knowing it was cowardly of her, 'Why don't we go back to the house? Maybe we could make some cocoa.' Cocoa had been her mother's cure for all childhood sorrows.

'I'll put the shovel away,' Daniel said. 'Oh, here's Dad.'

Jenny looked around. Graham was scarcely twenty feet away from them, his gaze intent upon the little group around the flower-bedecked grave. Both children ran for him, leaving Jenny abandoned under the beech tree. With a lump in her throat she watched him kneel and gather them in, heard Gillie finally, begin to cry, and felt a painful, demeaning stab of jealousy.

Then Graham looked up, meeting Jenny's eyes squarely. He said very simply, across the distance that separated them, 'Thank you, Jenny,' but he said it in such a way that her jealousy vanished.

She watched silently as Graham hugged his children, wiped Gillie's nose and eventually stood up. 'I think Jenny's idea of cocoa was a good one. Mrs Layton made a chocolate cake, too. We'll have some of that.'

'It'll ruin our appetite,' Daniel sniffed.

'That's right, it will,' his father said cheerfully. 'Coming?'

'Jenny, too,' declared Gillie, bottom lip out-thrust.

'Jenny, too,' Graham agreed.

When they trooped into the kitchen, the children and Jenny minus their shoes, Mrs, Layton had gone. Jenny looked around, eyebrows raised. Graham said, 'She leaves promptly at five. So I always get home from work by then.'

Jason waddled in from the living room, saw Jenny, and greeted her with his usual ecstatic, 'Dadada.' She picked him up and carried on a conversation with him more noted for repetition than intelligibility as the others cut a luscious-looking chocolate cake and made mugs of frothy cocoa topped with marshmallows. The impromptu picnic in the big, old-fashioned kitchen hit exactly the right note. By the time the chocolate cake had disappeared, the tears had dried on Gillie's cheeks and Daniel did not look quite so downcast. Graham said, 'Late supper today. Off you go and play for a while.'

Jason was sitting on the floor stuffing crumbs into his mouth, Aware of the silence, Jenny gathered up the mugs and carried them over to the sink, which overlooked the garden.

'I'll do that,' Graham said.

'No, that's——'

He stayed her with a hand on her wrist. 'You've done enough for one day. Jenny, you handled the whole situation beautifully.'

She stared down at his hand. 'I've probably undermined all their Sunday school training.'

'You gave a sense of dignity to the death of a creature they both loved—you couldn't have done more. I'm only sorry you had to cope with—with what you must have found on the street.'

'I'm glad I was there. I don't think Mrs Layton would have been much help.'

'When it comes to things like scraped knees—or dead cats—Mrs Layton is apt to retreat to the kitchen. But she genuinely likes the children, and that's worth such a lot . . . you like them, too, Jenny, don't you? You'll make a good mother some day.'

'Oh, yes,' Jenny said, and could not mask the pain in her voice, 'I like them. I've got to go, Graham, Lois invited me over for a barbecue. You know Lois Turnbull, don't you?'

Graham disregarded her question for the red herring it was. 'I touched a nerve there, didn't I, Jenny? I'm sorry, I certainly didn't mean to.'

'It doesn't matter,' she said, her tone warding off his concern.

'I'm beginning to think it matters a great deal.'

She gazed at him, panic-stricken, and remembered Marc's fumbled explanation and Samuel's cold denial. 'I've really got to go—I'm late as it is.'

'What are you running from?'

She tugged her wrist from his grasp. 'You. Men. Marriage. Children,' she said wildly. 'Will that do for a start?'

'Why? What happened?'

'Say goodbye to the children for me.'

He said grimly, 'You can't run for ever, Jenny.'

She stuck out her chin. 'I'll run as far and as fast as I wish.'

'My legs are longer than yours—so sooner or later I'll catch up with you.'

'Make it later,' she retorted rudely.

'Sooner sounds a better idea to me. When you pout like that, you look like Gillie in one of her moods. Jenny——' The smile faded from his face. 'Why have you never married? What went wrong? Because something did, I know.'

'I don't want to discuss it! And you can't blame me for that—you've scarcely been open with me about Gillie's piano lessons, have you? Graham, I should have been at Lois's fifteen minutes ago.'

'You'll tell me—and soon. In the meantime, let me thank you again for everything you did today. I can't think of anyone who would have managed more capably or with more sensitivity than you.'

Jenny could feel herself blushing; the power of sensible speech seemed to have deserted her. 'Goodbye,' she gasped and fled for the door. She did remember to pick up her books from the grass.

A couple of minutes later, sitting in her car which was still parked outside the Music building, Jenny looked at her watch and her skirt in equal dismay. The barbecue was at six o'clock: her watch said twenty past. Her skirt, a floral print, was stained with both mud and blood, and, as she had been doing ever since she had knelt in the road outside Graham's house, she hastily blanked from her mind the image of Snowflake's mangled body. Wrenching her thoughts back to practicalities, she knew she did not have the time to go home and change; surely Lois was a good enough friend to take her as she was? Jenny turned the key in the ignition and backed out on the street.

She drew up against the kerb in front of Lois's house behind a racy scarlet sports car. Five minutes in the bathroom to clean up and a good strong drink would do wonders for her morale, she decided, as she ran up the front path and pressed the doorbell.

The man who opened the door was a complete stranger. Jenny gaped at him, registering that he was tall, good-looking and extremely self-assured. But before she could say anything he remarked pleasantly, 'You must be Jenny—do come in. Terry's muttering imprecations over the barbecue coals, which are not behaving as they should, and Lois is up to her wrists in a tossed salad.'

Since Lois never did anything by half-measures, Jenny had to laugh. Mentally trying to switch gears from Graham Tyson and his children, she held out her hand. 'Jenny Sprague.'

'Max Carey. I'm a new arrival in Brockton, but I've known Terry for years—we went to high school together. I was given orders to take you to the kitchen.'

Lois, who was dashingly attired in a lime green jumpsuit with earrings that dangled nearly to her shoulders, was pouring dressing over the salad. 'Hello, darling,' she cried. 'You met Max, did you? Jenny, what *have* you been doing? You've got mud all over your face.'

'Surely not *all* over?' Jenny chided. 'It's a long story, for the telling of which I need a drink.'

'Vodka, rum, red wine or beer?' Max said promptly.

'Rum and Coke, please.' Jenny perched herself on a stool, arranging her skirt so the stains were not too glaringly obvious, and proceeded to describe the demise of Snowflake. 'So by the time I left Graham's I was already twenty minutes late,' she finished. 'I should have gone home to change, I guess.'

'You look wonderful,' Max declared. He tore off a piece of paper towel, dampened it under the tap and advanced on Jenny. 'Hold still.'

She obliged, gazing at him with limpid eyes as he

rubbed the offending mud from her face. He really was
extremely good-looking . . . and didn't he know it!

Lois, who was devoid of tact, said grumpily, 'The last
thing you need is to get involved with Graham Tyson
and his four children.'

Since this was precisely what Jenny had been telling
herself, it was illogical of her to feel annoyed that Lois
should arrive at the same conclusion. 'Three,' she
defended.

'Three what?' said Lois peevishly.

'Three children. He only has three.'

'Only? Really, Jenny——'

'Would you have preferred me to have left the
children to cope with the very squashed remains of their
cat? On their own?'

Fortunately Terry chose this moment to come in from
the garden through the screen door. 'The damn thing
finally caught,' he said. 'Hi, Jenny, how's it going? Did
you drain the marinade off the steak, Lois?'

Terry was Lois's height but twice her girth. He was a
quick-tempered man with a crisp black beard who
played the trumpet brilliantly whether drunk or sober.
He and Lois had never established to their lasting
satisfaction which of them was the boss in their
marriage, so fought frequently and uninhibitedly, a
pastime they both seemed to enjoy.

Lois said smugly, 'Of course I did,' and indicated the
platter of raw, red meat.

Jenny gulped and looked away in time to hear Terry
say, 'Where the hell did you hide the barbecue tongs,
Lois? They're supposed to be by the back door.'

'No, they're not——'

Max turned his back on them and said *sotto voce* to
Jenny, 'What's Lois got against this Tyson character?'

Jenny decided to be direct. 'She thinks he has too
many children. She's trying to marry me off, you see.'

Lois and Terry had disappeared, arguing, down the

basement steps in search of the barbecue tools. 'I
gathered as much, our Lois not being the soul of
discretion. I'm the next candidate, as I'm sure you
realise. I think you're quite astonishingly beautiful and
I'd very much like to see you again, but I might as well
tell you right now that I am not interested in marriage.'

Jenny laughed, beginning to like him. 'That suits me
fine. Because neither am I.'

'We shall have to compare reasons.' He cocked his
head as Lois clattered up the steps. 'Some other time.'

Jenny enjoyed the evening, for the food was delicious
and the talk lively. Max was a geologist, a specialist in
micro-fossils, in pursuit of which he had had some
amazing and bizarre adventures which lost nothing in
the telling. Jenny drank rather more than was good for
her, and at midnight an impromptu sing-song took
place, followed by Terry playing the trumpet with a
complete disregard for the sleeping patterns of his
neighbours. Jenny had a hangover the next day, which
she accepted philosophically since it was so well-
deserved.

Her telephone began to ring more frequently as
September and the beginning of classes approached.
Some were business calls, Dr Moorhead revealing
himself to be a fussy and authoritative administrator;
but others were social. Max she saw often and always
with enjoyment. She knew he had an affair in mind and
had the feeling that when she said no she would see less
of him, which, if understandable, would be a pity.

Occasionally she went canoeing with Roland; and as
other Faculty members came back to town after the
summer break, she was invited to a number of parties.
At none of them did she see Graham Tyson. He had not
phoned to invite her anywhere.

Gillie, however, phoned at least once a week. One
sunny Tuesday afternoon, the week before school
started, she came for a visit.

Jenny had been sunbathing on the back porch, justifying her laziness by listening to tapes by Schnabel and Horowitz. Her first indication of Gillie's presence was the intervention of a pair of slim, socked ankles into her field of vision. Startled, she looked up. 'Oh, hi, Gillie.' She switched off the cassette player and removed the earphones. 'I didn't hear you arrive . . . you didn't walk, did you?'

Gillie was wearing blue shorts and a halter top, her bleached hair in a ponytail. 'I bicycled,' she said.

'Along the highway? Are you allowed to do that?'

The child looked acutely uncomfortable and said nothing.

'You're not,' Jenny concluded. 'We'll put your bike in the back of my car and I'll drive you home.' Gillie's face fell, so Jenny added hastily, 'But now that you're here, we might as well have a visit. Come in—you must be thirsty.'

'It was hard work going up the hills,' Gillie admitted.

In the kitchen Jenny mixed frozen orange juice and put some home-made cookies on a plate. She also pulled on a loose shirt over her bikini. 'Let's go into the other room.'

The living room with its high ceilings and graceful plants gave the impression of coolness. Gillie chattered away as she drank her juice. Daniel had started soccer practice, and Jason had added out, down, and cookie to his vocabulary. 'He'd like these,' Gillie said, helping herself to another chocolate chip cookie. 'Daniel wants us to get a kitten because of poor Snowflake being dead, but so far Dad says no, he's got problems enough. You'll take me home before Dad gets back from work, will you, Jenny?'

'I'm meeting Dr Moorhead at four o'clock, so I will, yes. But I don't want to be party to deceiving your father, Gillie—if you're not allowed to bicycle on the highway, you mustn't do it again. Maybe we could arrange that I could bring you out here for supper every now and then.'

'That would be nice.' Gillie looked over at the grand piano in the alcove. 'I memorised two new pieces—shall I play them for you? They're called *Hopscotch* and *Sailor's Dance*.'

Jenny recognised the titles, because they were two of the pieces she had used at music camp to capture Kevin's interest; they were not, however, enough of a challenge for Gillie. 'They're fun to play, aren't they?' she said diplomatically.

Gillie played them with skill and verve. After suggesting a few minor corrections, Jenny had her play some Beethoven and Bach. 'Your pedalling isn't quite right there.' She sat down beside Gillie. 'The staccato must be absolutely crisp and sharp. Like this, Then *hold* that chord . . . one, two, three . . . now you try.'

So when Graham Tyson walked into the living room five minutes later Jenny and his daughter were side by side on the piano bench and the Beethoven *Bagatelle* was being torn apart bar by bar. He said in a tight, angry voice, 'How long has this being going on?'

As Gillie hit a discord Jenny swung around, her shirt falling open to reveal the extreme brevity of her bikini. Graham had his hands thrust in his pockets. His shoulders were hunched. One did not have to possess great powers of perception to realise he was in a towering rage. 'How did you get in?' exclaimed Jenny.

'Through the front door.'

'Haven't you heard of an invention called a doorbell?'

'My daughter's bike is lying on the grass. I heard the piano playing. I did not consider that I needed a gilt-edged invitation to enter.'

'I'm not talking about gilt-edged invitations—I'm talking about common politeness!'

'In which you could certainly do with a lesson or two. Or is it normal practice with you, Miss Sprague, to encourage young children to break their parents' rules and endanger their lives on the highway? Not to mention the actual deception that this piano lesson involves. I did ask you how long this has been going on!'

Jenny stood up, choosing to ignore Gillie's sensibilities and her own near-nakedness. 'You're jumping to all the wrong conclusions!'

'Did Gillie ride her bicycle out here or did she not?'

'She did, yes. But——'

'And were you or were you not involved in a piano lesson when I arrived?'

'It was not planned,' Jenny said in a clipped voice.

'Whether murder is premeditated or unpremeditated, the victim is just as dead.'

'Oh, do *stop*!' Jenny cried.

He disregarded her. 'Gillie, here are the car keys. Go out and put your bike in the trunk, and then wait outside. I won't be long.'

'Dad——'

'Do as I say!'

Silent tears were trickling down Gillie's face. She took the keys from her father's outstretched hand and stumbled out of the door. 'Now——' said Graham Tyson.

But Jenny had had enough. 'Now nothing!' she exploded. 'You listen to me, Graham Tyson! Gillie has never ridden her bicycle out here before and I have already told her she must not do so again. The first thing I knew about today's outing was when I looked up and there she was. Furthermore—kindly don't interrupt!—I can no more prevent that child from playing the piano than I can stop her from breathing, and the sooner you realise that the better. Nor was I wilfully deceiving you—that's not my style.' She ran out of breath and words simultaneously, and sat down hard on the piano bench.

'You have one hell of a temper!'

'The temper of a shrew—or so an acquaintance of mine once said.'

'I'm damned if I'll be looked on as an acquaintance!' he snarled.

Acquaintanceship did not seem the right word to describe the complicated bond between her and Graham Tyson. Jenny gave him a dirty look. 'I don't understand how you knew Gillie was here.'

'Gillie had a dentist's appointment this afternoon that I'd forgotten about. After the receptionist phoned me, I went home to get her. Mrs Layton said she'd gone off on her bicycle. I've spent the last two hours scouring the roads, becoming more and more convinced I was going to find her dead in the ditch.'

Although he had spoken without emotion, Jenny was not deceived. She said drily, 'Anger is a typical response to the cessation of extreme anxiety.'

'I guess I owe you an apology.'

'I don't need one. Gillie does.'

'I'll talk to Gillie on the way home. Jenny——'

Without another word being spoken they suddenly found themselves locked in each other's arms in the middle of the room, kissing each other as if they had just invented kissing. Graham strained her to him, his hands digging into her flesh under her shirt. As she felt his instant arousal, she made a tiny sound deep in her throat expressive of pleasure, gratification and passionate hunger and buried her fingers in the thickness of his hair.

They did not decorously release one another; they fell apart, panting. 'My God!' muuttered Graham.

It seemed an entirely appropriate comment to Jenny. She drew a long, shuddering breath. 'How did that happen?' she said faintly.

He swallowed, and with a fascination so erotic as to border on indecency she watched the muscles move in his throat. He ventured, 'Your state of near-nudity?'

"*You're* fully dressed!'

'If it were not for Gillie, the dentist's appointment and a dozen other concerns, I would much prefer not to be.'

Her smile was provocative, 'I can only reciprocate that.'

'Somehow I thought you would.' The light left his eyes. 'It won't do, Jenny. Goddammit, it won't do.'

'Why not?' she said bluntly.

'Because I'm not into one-night stands ... and neither, I would guess, are you.'

'No, I guess I'm not.' But why would it have to be a one-night stand? She pulled the edges of her shirt together, hugging her breasts. 'You'll be late for the dentist.'

'Damn and blast the dentist!' His scowl was self-derisory. 'Normally I am not a man given to profanity—yet another of the effects you have upon me.'

She remembered the very obvious effect of two or three minutes ago and mumbled, 'Gillie's probably out there still crying.'

Frustration bit into his features, 'Yeah ... she probably is. I've got to go—take care, Jenny.' He wheeled and strode across the room. The door banged shut behind him. A few minutes later Jenny heard a car engine start.

She stood still in the middle of the room, feeling a strong urge to indulge in a good cry herself. Instead, of necessity, she got dressed and endeavoured to prepare herself for the punctiliousness of Dr Moorhead.

Two days later Jenny saw Graham again, a meeting very nearly as frustrating as the one she had privately labelled The Row at the House. Max had phoned and suggested they go to Shediac for a swim and a barbecue. Because her mind had been preoccupied with the emotional inconsistencies of Graham Tyson to the exclusion of piano pedagogy, she agreed immediately. Anyone would do as a distraction, and Max with his blond good looks and sense of fun was far from just anyone. She dressed in green shorts and top with matching sandals of which Lois would approve, and saw appreciation and a healthy degree of lust in Max's eyes when he came to the door. He had not yet invited her to stay overnight at his place or asked to stay at hers, but she sensed such an offer would not be long in coming. Being a perfectly normal female, she enjoyed his company. However, she never once felt like attacking him and hauling him off to bed, the response Graham seemed to evoke simply by being in the same room with her. Sexual desire was as inconsistent and difficult to fathom as Graham himself, she decided, smiling at Max. 'You look very nice,' she said cordially, and so he did, in white canvas shorts and a vaguely nautical T-shirt, his sunglasses pushed back on to his hair.

'Thank you. May I return the compliment?'

She giggled, 'You stroke my ego and I'll stroke yours. I've got home-made cookies, please note the word home-made, fruit and a salad.'

'I've got the wine and the rolls, and we'll pick up the steak downtown. Have you got a jacket and maybe some jeans? It can get cool by the water.'

'Mmm. And a towel, suntan lotion, a sunhat, a book and a beach ball. As well as plates, knives and forks and glasses.'

'The simple life.'

'I hate people who go to Europe for three weeks with one small suitcase.'

He looked at the pile of paraphernalia. 'If you need all this for a picnic in Shediac, you'd need your own ocean liner for three weeks in Europe!'

She pulled a face at him, and in perfect harmony with each other they loaded up the car and set off for the grocery store. They were standing in front of the meat display, Max with his arm casually looped around her shoulders, Jenny laughing at some remark he had made, when behind them a boy called, 'Hi, Jenny!' and another voice yelled, 'Dadada!'

Still in the circle of Max's arm, Jenny turned around. Jason was strapped into the grocery cart which Graham was pushing. Gillie and Daniel were glowering at Max in a manner not difficult to interpret. Graham's frown was somewhat less conspicuous, but scarcely to be ignored.

Dog in the manger, Jenny addressed him silently. Maybe I'd rather be doing groceries with you than going to the beach with Max. But if you don't ask me, then I don't have a choice, do I? She smiled in a general way at all four of them and said, 'Hello.'

'Who're you?' Daniel said, rudely, to Max.

Graham's, 'Mind your manners, Daniel,' coincided with Max's, 'My name is Max Carey. I'm a geologist, and I've just moved here. Who are you?'

Quickly Jenny intervened. 'Max, this is the Tyson family. Graham, who's head of the History Department, and his children—Jason in the seat, and Daniel and Gillie. How are you, Graham?'

'Fine,' he said briefly. 'Max and I met yesterday at the Faculty club.'

'So we did,' said Max, then asked a polite question about the beginning of classes, which Graham began to answer just as politely. Jenny listened in silence, inevitably struck by the constrast between the two men. Graham, wearing a striped shirt and light grey trousers, was surrounded in a very obvious way by all his responsibilities. Max, on the other hand, could have graced the cover of a yachting magazine; he was probably about the same age as Graham, but looked much younger. Carefree, thought Jenny. Max was, literally, care-free, and intended to remain so.

Jason began struggling against the straps that held him in the cart, grunting with exertion. 'I'd better go,' Graham said, his smile somehow passing over Jenny without really including her. 'See you around, Max. 'Bye, Jenny.'

Gillie, who had not said hello, did not say goodbye, either. Her scowl would have withered a lesser man than Max. As it was, Max said goodbye to the children individually, remembering each name. The Tyson family continued on their way and Max picked out two T-bone steaks from the rack. 'These look okay. Enough for you?'

'Heavens, yes!'

'Let's go.'

He paid for the steaks and they left the store. Max threw the meat in the cooler in the back of the car and got in beside Jenny. 'That man's in love with you,' he said.

Jenny had been polishing her sunglasses. She very deliberately perched them on her nose, adjusting the ear-pieces, and said, 'Funny joke. Please laugh here.'

Max engaged the clutch and swung out into the traffic. 'I'm not joking. Yesterday he was extremely pleasant, and today when he saw me with you he was barely civil.'

'You're confusing him with Daniel. Daniel's the one who was rude.'

'And the little blonde girl—what was her name? Gillie. If they could have put me on a spaceship to Mars, they would have. They obviously see you as the next Mrs Tyson. What happened to the first one, by the way?'

'She died.'

'Worn out by childbirth, I should think. I thought Lois told me there were four children.'

'Three,' Jenny said in exasperation. 'And it's perfectly acceptable to have more than one child.'

'You sound very much on the defensive.' He gave her a lazy smile. 'Are you in love with him, Jenny?'

'No!'

'Tell the truth, sugarplum—I can take it like a man.'

'Oh Max, do stop!' Jenny cried, torn between anger and laughter. 'I'm not in love with Graham, of course I'm not, but even if I were you wouldn't care. *You're* not in love with me!'

'Nope,' he agreed, adding with unaccustomed seriousness, 'I don't suppose I'll ever fall in love with anyone, doesn't seem to suit my nature. But I like you, I enjoy your company, and I want to take you to bed.'

He was turning on to the main highway. Jenny preserved a judicious silence until the red sports car had merged into the flow of traffic. Then she said, 'I know. I read the signs. But——'

'But you're in love with Graham Tyson.'

She frowned down at her fingers. 'Seriously, Max, I'm not. How could I be? I've never even had a proper date with him. The first time I was at his house we had a fight. The only time he's been to my house we had a fight. In between I buried his kids' cat. I'm not in love with him.'

Max said carefully, 'You mean he's never asked you for a date?'

'That's right. Do you think I should write to Dear Abbie for advice? Maybe there's something my best friends aren't telling me.'

'Jenny darling, there's no need for false modesty. You're a gorgeous woman—and a very nice woman. The man's crazy.'

'The man's got three children.'

'Has he not heard of babysitters?'

'Oh, the children aren't really the issue. It's just that we fight all the time.'

'What about?' he asked curiously.

'Gillie's piano lessons mostly—I want her to have

lessons, she's a born pianist, and for some reason Graham won't allow it.'

'Hmm . . .' Max drove a few minutes in silence, then said, 'Well, I'm not about to wallow in altruism, Jenny, and back off our friendship because of Graham Tyson. I like dating you and I think you like dating me . . .'

As he paused, she said obligingly, 'I do—you're fun.'

'And if Mr Tyson hasn't got the wit to pick up the phone and ask you out, that's his problem.'

Jenny knew wit had nothing to do with Graham's attitude, but wisely held her peace. She had revealed enough of her inner confusion as it was. 'A swim is going to feel good,' she said. 'I spent four hours in the library today trying to trace some references I needed. It turns out I'll have to use inter-library loan—could take weeks!'

Max accepted the change of subject and Graham was not mentioned again. They arrived at the beach. The flat stretch of sand, the invigorating chill of the waves, the delicious scent of the sizzling steaks and the splash of colour as the sun sank to the horizon all delighted Jenny, and if she had any thoughts that Graham's children would also have enjoyed them, she kept these thoughts to herself.

CHAPTER FIVE

THE following weekend, the last before classes began, Max went home to Prince Edward Island to visit his parents; contrary to his carefully cultivated playboy image, he was devoted to all the members of his large family. He had not suggested Jenny go with him. 'Mum wants to marry me off as badly as Lois wants to do the same for you. If I took a woman home with me for the weekend, she'd have us marching up to the altar by Sunday with all my sisters cheering her on.'

'Which would definitely ruin your bachelor status!'

'Not to mention my lifestyle.' He kissed her firmly and with considerable expertise. 'Wait for me, won't you, love of my heart? We could play tennis on Tuesday evening. After facing the unwashed student hordes all day, we'll need to bash a ball around.'

'It's a date.'

So Tuesday evening at six o'clock found Jenny and Max in tennis whites strolling down the main street of Brockton, each with a bag of gear, eating large ice cream cones and chattering away with the ease of people who like each other.

'Did you see Graham Tyson at the weekend?' Max asked.

'Are you kidding? No.'

'Why don't *you* call *him* up and ask for a date?'

She crunched into the cone. 'No to that, too.'

'Then you'll have to take out your frustrations on the tennis court.'

Gloomily she replied, 'Do you think we always want what we can't have?'

Max glanced around to make sure no one was within

earshot, and said self-righteously, 'I shall never allow you into my bed.'

Jenny began to laugh. 'Reverse psychology. Let's play tennis.'

'Rejected again!'

'Max——' she began, the laughter dying from her face.

'Don't panic, Jenny. When you're ready, it'll happen. Being a man of strong appetites,' he leered down at her bosom, 'I hope it'll be soon. But I can wait.'

She felt a rush of affection for him. 'I'm lucky to have you for a friend.'

'Of course you are! Let's take the far court, I haven't played much this summer and the fewer people who see my mistakes, the better.'

He was—not to Jenny's surprise—a very good player. She won only one of the three sets, but did get rid of some of the frustration that the thought of Graham Tyson always seemed to engender.

Afterwards they had a beer in the club house, then went their separate ways. Jenny was walking back down the main street, idly swinging her racquet, when a car pulled up alongside her. A BMW, she saw with a confusing mixture of excitement, trepidation and—unmistakably—joy.

Graham Tyson got out. His jeans were faded from many washings and clung to his lean hips, while his equally faded blue shirt emphasised the intense blue of his eyes. 'Where's Max?' he said with more than usual abruptness.

She tried to smother the joy and raised her brows. 'How do you know I was with Max?'

'I drove by earlier and saw you playing.'

Swishing her racquet back and forth through the air, she murmured, 'I would have thought you had better things to do than follow me around.'

His raised eyebrow was a replica of her own. 'How

could I have? . . . Is he coming back?'

'No. And I'm going home.'

'No, you're not. You're coming for a drive.'

'I'm not one of your children whom you can order around!'

'That statement demonstrates an inspired grasp of the truth . . . as I believe you once said to me.'

'Are you the kind of person who holds a grudge?' she asked suspiciously.

'Not at all. I just happen to remember everything you've ever said to me!'

The joy came bubbling up again. With an attempt at severity, Jenny asked. 'Am I supposed to be impressed?'

'I hope so. Do come for a drive, Jenny—there's something I want to tell you.'

She gazed at him through her lashes. 'What if I refuse?'

'I shall pick you up, throw you in the car and drive off into the sunset.'

She looked disparagingly at the BMW. 'It should be a coal-black steed.'

'And I a knight in shining armour . . . although when I think of being encased in a suit of armour, I'm heartily glad I live in the twentieth century.'

Her curiosity was nearly killing her. 'What do you want to tell me about?'

'You'll find out when you get there.'

'Then what are we waiting for?' she said demurely.

He leaned forward and in magnificent unconcern for all the other pedestrians on Main Street gave her a quick, hard kiss. Then he opened the car door. As Jenny got in, not for anything could she have prevented the smile on her lips.

Graham drove in a direction Jenny had never been before, to a bluff south of the town that overlooked the sweep of the marshes and the faraway gleam of the bay.

The herds of cattle looked like small red and white toys; in the setting sun the shadows of the squat grey barns were elongated like those of skyscrapers. Graham turned off the motor and they got out, walking to the edge of the bluff. They had the place to themselves.

He turned to face her, his back to the sun, his features in shadow; what he said to her was all the more forceful because he spoke so quietly, though it was characteristic of him to plunge right in. 'Jenny, meeting you has thrown my whole life in a turmoil. I was content until you came along—doing my work, bringing up my children, dating occasionally—everything on a nice even keel and under control.' He gave her a twisted smile. 'Control is scarcely descriptive of my feelings when I'm anywhere near you . . . The other thing you've done, of course, is to bring me up short as far as Gillie's talent for the piano is concerned. And that's really what I want to talk to you about.'

Jenny gazed up at him. He had not, as yet, told her anything she had not guessed, but the putting of his feelings into words made them more real, more solid, and, in an inexplicable way, frightening.

'There's a reason behind my refusal to allow Gillie piano lessons.' His voice roughened. 'A very personal reason. You see, my father was a pianist, Jenny, and the demands of his career dominated my childhood. He was a good pianist, but not good enough to make it to the top. And that was something he was never able to accept. He practised like a madman, he haunted the agencies, his tours were a nightmare, and a bad review could send him into despair; as he got older the tours went from second-rate to third-rate to fourth-rate . . . he died of a heart attack at the age of fifty. I was almost glad, because for him the struggle was over. Maybe my mother was glad as well, I don't know. She had a hard life all those years, moving around the country, working to supplement his income, trying to shield my sister and me from his debilitating attacks of depression ... His career cost him his life, Jenny, and I can't bear to think of Gillie being subjected to the same pressures.' He made a tiny, helpless gesture with his hands, his eyes bleak. 'I love Gillie. I want the best for her. It would kill me to see in her that same despair.'

He had finished. Jenny reached over and rested her hand on his arm, her eyes filled with tears. 'I'm sorry about your father, Graham. And I see why you couldn't tell me about him earlier. You don't tell a complete stranger that kind of thing, do you?'

Some of the bleakness left his eyes. 'I hoped you'd understand.'

'But Gillie isn't the same as your father, Graham. She's a person in her own right.'

'I know that. And I realise I've been making a decision that's not mine to make—imposing my own hang-ups on my daughter.' The words were torn from him. 'Do you think *she* could make it to the top, Jenny?'

'I don't know. It's too early to tell. She has an inborn intuition for music, and she's desperate to learn ... I think she could could go a very long way.'

He thrust his hands in his pockets and stared out over the golden marshes. 'My father's life was a hell on earth.'

And he made yours hell as well, Jenny thought. 'You're a good man, Graham, and a fine parent,' she said urgently. 'You're giving Gillie the stability and love that will enable her to handle whatever the future brings—the balance so that if she can't make it to the top, she will accept that knowledge with grace and courage.'

'I've thought of that, too. But how can I *know*?'

'You can't. Gillie is a separate person who will have to make her own mistakes.' She paused. 'I went through a very bad time when my own limitations really struck home, the summer I was twenty-one. But my father had always instilled in me the belief that you do the best you can and that's all you can do. Gillie, because she has a greater gift than I, and so will come closer to the top, may have a more difficult time if she doesn't succeed.'

Graham was still staring out the marshes. 'But I must give her that freedom of choice.'

'I think so ... Have you ever told her about your father?' He shook his head. 'Tell her, Graham. She's exceptionally sensitive for a child her age. It will help her to understand.'

With one hand he rubbed the tension from the back of his neck. 'Yeah ... you see, until you came along, I hadn't realised how important music was to her. I thought she just had the usual little girl's urge for lessons.' He produced a wry smile. 'One of the reasons I reacted against you so strongly was your choice of profession. Another pianist. The last thing I needed!'

Jenny, who had talked so volubly in Gillie's cause, could now find no words. With one hand Graham stroked her cheek. 'Thank you for hearing me out,' he said.

She had seen in him anger and laughter, passion and fierce resentment, but never the tenderness that now softened his strong features and darkened his eyes. It melted any vestige of anger against him. She wanted that tenderness to last for ever. She wanted to be taken into his arms and held, to offer him the comfort of human touch. She wanted to be kissed until she forgot everything but the naked drive of desire for a man's hard body ...

'No, Jenny,' he said thickly. 'Not yet. We can't.'

She tried to make a joke of it. 'Am I that easily read?'

'I know you—I've told you that before. We'd better leave. This is far too beautiful a place and we're much too obviously alone, and when you look at me like that all my good intentions vanish. Is your car in town?'

'Yes,' she stumbled. 'Yes, it is.' But I don't want to go

back to town, she thought with frantic honesty. I don't want to leave.

She did not say so. She sat in the car and ten minutes later they were back on the main street in Brockton. Graham's kiss landed on her cheek. 'Take care, Jenny. I'll see you soon.'

She tried to smile, picked up her gear and climbed out. As he drove away she stood still on the pavement and felt loneliness of an intensity that terrified her.

The beginning of classes immersed Jenny in a round of activity. She had done some part-time teaching in New York, so had a measure of experience to counter her initial nervousness; being blessed with a realistic sense of her own capabilities as well as a sense of humour, she soon established a rapport with most of her students. There were always those only interested in learning their capacity for beer and late hours, but to counterbalance, there were the few who loved music as much as Jenny did, and who were consequently a delight to teach. She settled into her office, which by a stroke of fortune faced the rose garden, and started to feel at home, relishing the challenge of young minds and the bustle of the students' presence.

She continued to see Max, to lose at tennis and to stay out of his bed. She ran on the marshes in the hazy light of evening and every second day swam at the University pool. She thought about Graham more than was good for her.

A week after their drive out to the bluff, he came to see her.

Earlier in the evening Jenny had gone for a run. She had showered afterwards and dressed in a cerise silk robe, belting it about her waist and piling her hair on top of her head. Settling herself at the dining-room table, she was soon absorbed in marking a test she had unexpectedly given her piano pedagogy course, a test which for many of them had plainly come as an unpleasant surprise.

At first she thought she had imagined the knock at the door. She frowned at the clock, which said ten minutes to ten. But then she heard it again: the impatient knock of someone who would not be ignored.

She had lived in New York long enough that she called through the closed door, 'Who's there?'

'Graham.'

Jenny looked in faint dismay at her ink-stained fingers and tried to slow the erratic pounding of her heart. Then she opened the door.

Graham stared down at her. In the soft fall of light from the other room her hair shone gold. The cerise robe, long-sleeved, full-length, covered her more than adequately yet clung at breast and hip and rustled when she moved. Her eyes were full of uncertainty.

He swallowed. 'May I come in? Is Max here?'

'No, he isn't.' She moved back a pace. 'What would you have done if he had been?'

He stepped over the threshold and closed the door. 'Kicked him out.'

Her heart was now galloping rather than bounding. 'You talk a good line, Graham Tyson! Don't you know it's customary to phone someone before you visit them at ten o'clock at night?'

Graham's grin was boyish. 'Don't be mad at me, Jenny. An elderly neighbour of mine dropped in with some home-made jam, and because it's such a beautiful night she suggested I go out for walk while she stayed with the children. I didn't even stop to think—I came straight out here. I hadn't realised it was as late as ten.'

Nervously Jenny pulled her belt a little tighter. 'I'd love to go for a walk. I—I'll go and get changed.'

'Come here first.'

She should run. In the opposite direction, as far and as fast as she could . . . Instead she swayed towards him,

her eyes blind with need. There was nothing gentle in
his kiss, or in the way he seized and held her. As his
tongue parted her lips, his hands roamed her body, the
thin silk an added temptation rather than a barrier. He
had pulled her hips hard against his; her palms were
pressed into his back, her nails searching out the taut
muscle and ridges of bone beneath his shirt.

Then he loosened his hold enough to push back the
neckline of her gown. 'I want to look at you,' he said
huskily. 'May I, Jenny?'

'Yes. Oh, Graham, yes!'

In a soft whisper of silk the robe fell down her
shoulders. When he eased the sleeves down her arms,
the wide lapels opened to bare her breasts. He stood
very still, his eyes caressing her nudity, learning every
detail of the creamy flesh and taut, dusky nipples. Then
his fingers traced the same curves, his face rapt, its
fierceness lost in wonder. And Jenny felt tears gather in
her eyes and spill down her cheeks.

'Jenny—did I hurt you?' He clasped her bare
shoulders. 'Jenny dear, don't cry.'

'I can't help it. I—I feel so close to you.'

With infinite gentleness he wiped a teardrop from her
cheek. 'I wouldn't hurt you for the world. But, oh God, I
want to make love to you!'

She hesitated. 'There must have been someone since
your wife died . . .'

'No, Jenny. There's been no one since Mona died.'

She said carefully, 'There's been no one for me since
Marc, who was my fiancé, broke our engagement over a
year ago.' She had never gone to bed with Samuel.

'This is none of my business and you can tell me to get
lost, but not Max?'

'Not Max. I like him, we've had a lot of fun together,
but I don't feel with him the way I feel with you . . . you
look like a little kid who's just been given a Christmas
present.'

'I was so goddamned jealous and had absolutely no right to be. Are you always this honest, Jenny?'

'I've learned to be—I don't like playing games. People get hurt when you play games.'

'Marc hurt you.'

She stirred restlessly. 'Yes. But I'm not ready to talk about that yet.'

'You can trust me.'

'I'd like to think I could,' she whispered. But could she? She had trusted Marc, and he had left her; maybe Graham would do the same . . .

'What did he do to you, Jenny?'

She crossed her arms over her breast, her eyes defiant. 'I'm scared to trust you!'

His voice was uncompromising. 'Once before I told you that you can't run for ever.'

But what if you reject me? she thought in silent terror. Marc did. Samuel did. I couldn't bear it if you did as well.

More moderately Graham added, 'Don't look so frightened, Jenny. I can't force you to tell me anything you're not ready to share, you know that as well as I do.' He tweaked a strand of her hair. 'Now go and get dressed, that robe is altogether too distracting. We'll go for a good brisk walk and maybe that'll get my mind out of the bedroom. I wonder if you're feeling as frustrated as I am?'

She was grateful for the change of subject. 'Every bit, I'm sure,' she said firmly.

His eyes were suddenly serious. 'You want to make love as badly as I do, don't you?'

She managed a weak smile. 'My body isn't quite as obvious about it as yours, that's all.'

'Your body is beautiful.'

Jenny flushed the colour of the robe. 'I'll go and get

changed,' she babbled. 'Back in a minute,' and fled for
the stairs.

Graham's elderly neighbour had been right—it was a
glorious night. As Jenny and Graham strolled hand in
hand down the dirt track behind the house, a crescent
moon was edging coyly over the distant range of hills to
mingle with the stars, which hung low on the horizon.
The silence was broken only by the crunch of their
footsteps in the gravel and by the sound of their voices.

Jenny talked about her childhood on the prairies, and
Graham told her about his sister Helen who lived in
Toronto; as they crossed between tall ranks of corn on
the one side and a field of wheat on the other, they
discussed the various universities where they had taken
their degrees. 'I married Mona two days after I got my
Ph.D.,' Graham finished matter-of-factly. 'Gillie was
born a year later.'

'Your wife must have been very young when she
died,' Jenny ventured.

'Not quite thirty. It was when Jason was born.'

'But why did she die, Graham? I didn't think women
died in childbirth any more.'

'She had a lot of very serious problems while she was
carrying Gillie—she developed a blood clot that
travelled to her lung. Pulmonary embolism is the
technical term, I'm sure you've heard of it. It placed her
at high risk both during the pregnancy and when she
gave birth, and as a consequence she was warned not to
get pregnant again. But Mona was an intensely
maternal woman and resented bitterly being told she
couldn't have more children—that's one of the reasons
we adopted Daniel, I thought it would take some of the
pressure off.' His voice thinned. 'She should never have
got pregnant with Jason ... she stopped using birth
control but chose not to tell me so. The doctors wanted
her to have an abortion, but she took the no doubt

admirable moral stance that abortion was murder. So
instead she died, as a direct result of Jason's birth . . . I
never understood Mona. Never.'

'But you loved her.'

'I don't even know that any more, Jenny. I did when I
married her. But Gillie's birth seemed to change her.
When we were told we must adopt children rather than
having more of our own, she shut me out, as though I
was no longer of any use to her. It sounds very petty if I
say I used to resent the love and attention she lavished
on the children . . . but I did. I suppose I should have
been suspicious when she suddenly warmed to me
before Jason was conceived; it's a measure of my
naïveté that I was merely happy, seeing a new warmth
in a marriage long gone cold.' He gave her a mirthless
smile. 'You understand why I value your honesty and
the way you refuse to play games?'

'Graham, I'm sorry,' Jenny whispered. 'I suppose I
assumed your marriage was happy—one does, doesn't
one, unless one's given evidence to the contrary. If she
was so devoted to the children, they must miss her
dreadfully.'

'They did, of course. But there was something
smothering in her devotion, at least I thought so. Even
when Gillie was very young, I used to wonder how
Mona would ever allow Gillie to become independent, a
person in her own right. Sounds disloyal, doesn't it?
We've made a shibboleth of not speaking ill of the dead
. . . perhaps because they're not here to defend
themselves.'

Since he had complimented her on her honesty,
Jenny took the risk of saying, 'Graham, because your
marriage was unhappy, are you afraid of ever re-
marrying?'

'No, I don't think so. I'm not afraid of marriage in
itself. I am afraid of the whole step-parenting scene;
I've seen a few second marriages go on the rocks

because of problems with the children. And, as I keep saying to you to the point of exhaustiveness—mostly in an effort to convince myself—I'm not into one-night stands.'

'Are you warning me off?' Jenny asked, her lightness of tone not wholly successful.

'I don't know, Jenny. I'll be honest—you've hit me like a ton of bricks and I'm still reeling from the shock. One part of me wants to pull you down in the grass right now, tear the clothes off you and make love to you. The other part, the sensible part, says slow down, Graham, think of the children, you can't act as if they don't exist ... what can you offer Jenny besides a whole host of problems related to children who aren't even hers?' A breath of wind rattled the corn. 'Yet when I'm with you I feel as though we belong together.'

She chose her words with care. 'I've been happier with you this evening walking across the marsh than I've ever been with Max.'

'Or with Marc?'

'Or with Marc,' she agreed slowly. 'You're right—there's a sense of belonging.'

He said with a simplicity that touched her, 'I was happier this evening than I've been for years.'

They had walked in a square and were now climbing the slope back towards the house. Jenny stopped to pull on a couple of heads of grass, thoughtfully chewing their soft, succulent stems. 'You're being hopelessly inaccurate if you think you're only offering me problems.'

But he had used the respite to withdraw into himself. 'I shouldn't have said that. Any of it. Forget it, will you, Jenny?'

'I don't know that I can.'

'Then try. Please.'

They had reached the pool of light cast by the back door light. 'So does that mean no more dates?' Jenny asked lightly, then looked over at him so quickly that she caught on his face all the pain and longing he might otherwise have masked. She answered her own question. 'Of course it doesn't . . . I'm assuming, of course, that tonight qualifies as a date.'

'Jenny——'

'We like each other, we enjoy each other's company, we're neither of us children.' She threw away the stems of grass. 'What's wrong with a date every now and then?'

'You're over-simplifying and you know it.'

'Perhaps you're over-complicating.'

'There's no such word.'

'I just invented it.'

Graham leaned against the back porch and was silent for what seemed to Jenny like a very long time. She could not read his expression; the circle of light in which they were standing seemed very small in the face of the darkness. Then, with the air of a man making a decision, he said, 'Will you invite me out here some evening and play for me? Chopin?'

Briefly she closed her eyes. 'There's nothing I would rather do.'

'Next week? I have to attend some meetings in Montreal at the weekend.'

'Monday evening I have a meeting. Tuesday? Come for a late dinner after the children have eaten.'

'Candlelight and music . . . sounds dangerous. I accept.' He leaned across and kissed her very gently..

The imprint of his lips lingered on her mouth, warm as the summer sun, making a mockery of the darkness. Yet she found herself thinking of Marc and Samuel, of Graham's three children, only two of whom were his, and of all her old inadequacies as a woman, and again felt how tiny was the circle of light in which they stood and how vast the darkness that surrounded them.

'Jenny, I must go, my neighbour will be thinking I've got lost. I'll see you next Tuesday. Seven-thirty or so?

That way at least Jason's in bed before I leave.'

'That's fine.'

'Goodnight . . . I'll be thinking about you.'

'I expect I'll do the same. Think about *you*, I mean.'

He raised one brow. 'Don't get into bed with Max.'

Jenny kept her face straight with an effort. 'Don't seduce any beautiful French girls.'

Solemnly he held out his hand. 'It's a deal.' But when she put her hand in his, instead of shaking it he raised it to his lips and kissed it, cradling it against his cheek as if he held something infinitely precious. 'Take care of yourself,' he said huskily. Then he turned on his heels, headed for the car, and a few seconds later had driven out of sight.

Jenny leaned against the doorpost and gazed up at the sky. The crescent moon was now hanging jauntily over her neigbour's barn. The stars twinkled in their eternal patterns, beautiful, cold and unreachable. I'm in love, she thought.

The stars did not change their courses. The heavens did not fall. She pulled a face, recognising how very trite it was to emote to the night skies, recognising also how ecstatically happy she felt. Graham had promised to think about her. That was all. But that was enough to make her spirit sing and to turn her heart to mush. She poked her tongue out at the stars and went indoors.

CHAPTER SIX

ON Saturday afternoon Max and Jenny drove into Halifax. Max's philosophy was that Brockton was a fine place to live as long as one got out of it every now and then, so he had purchased two tickets for the opening of the Nova Scotia Symphony and had told Jenny to put on what he called her glad rags. She was happy to oblige, partly from a genuine anticipation for the evening ahead, partly because the hours until Tuesday seemed to be passing incredibly slowly. One can only practise so much Chopin!

Her glad rags consisted of a silk dress and a lacy shawl. Max wore a pinstripe suit. She said smugly, 'We look very smart, wouldn't you agree?'

'Very. Let us hope that nobody else in Brockton has the same idea as us. I don't want to have to be polite to any professors, or intelligent, patient and reasonable with any students.'

'I'm a professor,' remarked Jenny.

He grinned at her. 'You're a distinct improvement over old Teasdale, whose opinions are as petrified as his fossils.'

Dr Emerson Teasdale was the geology department's counterpart to Dr Moorhead. 'I should hope I am,' said Jenny. 'This is fun, Max—what good ideas you have.'

He eyed her sideways. 'I have another idea. We could stay in Halifax overnight.'

She had wondered if he would suggest something of the kind. She considered such replies as 'But I don't have my toothbrush' or 'This is so sudden' and discarded them in favour of, 'I don't think so, Max. If you mean what I think you mean.'

'I most certainly do. One of the things I dislike about Brockton is the way everybody knows what everybody else is up to. No gossips in Halifax—or at least, none that know us. Don't look so worried, sugarplum. I shall ply you with strong drink and ask again. Later on. One of my mother's mottoes is that if at first you don't succeed, you try, try again.'

'I'm sure she didn't mean you to apply that to the seduction of female professors!'

He laughed. 'You're unquestionably right. I made a reservation for dinner at a little Italian restaurant that overlooks the harbour. I have a weakness for veal scallopini. Have you ever been to Europe, Jenny?'

He did not mention the subject of seduction again. The restaurant was small and intimate, their garlic shrimp and medallions of veal being the best Jenny had ever eaten. Between them she and Max consumed a bottle of wine, but the guest artist at the concert, a Spanish harpist, was not conducive to drowsiness. She talked very amusingly, in a charming accent, and she played exquisitely.

'Wonderful!' Jenny said, tucking her hand into Max's sleeve as they left the concert hall. 'Thank you so much, Max, I did enjoy that.'

Max had insisted that the concert was his treat, although he had not demurred when Jenny had split the bill for the meal, having recognised and accepted her strong streak of independence. 'A drink,' he said firmly. 'Terry recommended a bar in one of the new hotels.'

The bar had deep plush seats, dim lighting and a grand piano, which Jenny was eventually persuaded to play. She warmed up with some rags and Gershwin songs, then swung into Broadway hit tunes. At two a.m., when the bar closed, its occupants bade her farewell as if they had known and loved her for ever, and Max, who had proved to be the possessor of a very pleasant tenor voice, looped his arm around her shoulders. 'I had no idea you had such lowbrow tastes!'

'From Sibelius and Gluck to Simon and Garfunkel,' she giggled; for the past three hours she had been sipping on a drink that had sat on the piano and had been continually replenished by the grateful patrons of the bar.

'A woman of many talents,' he murmured, kissing her in a way she had no difficulty interpreting despite the never-empty drink. She thought, with extreme clarity, that life would probably be much simpler if she could spend the winter hopping in and out of bed with Max and forget all about Graham Tyson.

She said incoherently, 'I've had a fabulous evening, you're a super-attractive man and we're a long way from Brockton, but I can't do it, Max, I'm sorry. Just don't ask me to explain because I can't.'

'It's a long drive home,' Max reasoned, not quite ready to give up.

'How much have you had to drink?'

'Very little since dinner. I was saving myself for other things.'

He looked like a small boy about to be deprived of a treat rather than a man deprived of a lifelong passion. She remembered the strain and the longing in Graham's face and said, 'I'd really rather go home, Max.'

He stopped under one of the old-fashioned street lamps. 'We're not going to get it together, are we, Jenny?'

'I don't think we are,' she said truthfully.

'Graham?'

She pulled her shawl closer around her, for the wind off the harbour was cool. 'I'm not sleeping with him, if that's what you mean. We had what could qualify as a date last week and we have another planned for next week—but we're not going to fall into bed with each other ... Graham's scruples, not mine.'

'So you'd like to.'

She stared at his tie and said miserably, 'Yes.'

'I rather suspected as much.'

'I'm sorry if I've hurt you.'

'I'd rather you were honest—I guess—than get into bed with me wishing I was someone else.'

She tried to smile. 'I bet not many women turn you down.'

'Not many. It's good for me, I suppose. Keeps me humble. Well—we'd better head back.'

The sun had risen long before Max left Jenny at her house and continued on to his own. Because she had valiantly stayed awake the whole way home, she fell into bed and slept until noon, then was in bed again by nine o'clock that night. When she next woke up it was Monday. Lectures, lecture preparation, piano pupils and meetings took up the whole day. On Tuesday it poured with rain. Jenny smiled at all her students, laughed at Dr Moorhead's ponderous jokes and sang in the kitchen as she prepared dinner. She was deliriously happy. Quite possibly she should not be. Two dates do not a relationship make, she told herself sternly, an irrepressible smile on her face as she decorated the chocolate mousse with tiny slivers of toasted almonds sprinkled on whipped cream.

Graham arrived on time, for which she was deeply grateful; had he been five minutes late she would have wondered if he had died in a plane crash somewhere between Montreal and Brockton, or forgotten their date. She opened the door, gave him a dazzling smile and ushered him in, taking his raincoat and hanging it in the cupboard.

He was carrying half a dozen roses, all different colours, their stems untidily wrapped in tissue paper. 'The children wanted me to bring you something, so we picked these in the garden. The red one is from me.'

She raised them to her nostrils. 'They smell heavenly! The hothouse ones don't have any scent, do they? I'll

HARLEQUIN

♥ PRESENTS ♥

A Real Sweetheart of a Deal!

7 FREE GIFTS

PEEL BACK THIS CARD AND SEE WHAT YOU CAN GET! THEN...

Complete the Hand Inside ➤

It's easy! To play your cards right, just match this card with the cards inside.

Turn over for more details . . .

Incredible isn't it? Deal yourself in _right now_ and get 7 fabulous gifts. _ABSOLUTELY FREE._

1. 4 BRAND NEW HARLEQUIN PRESENTS NOVELS – FREE!
Sit back and enjoy the excitement, romance and thrills of fou
fantastic novels. You'll receive them as part of this winning streak

2. A BEAUTIFUL AND PRACTICAL PEN AND WATCH – FREE
This watch with its leather strap and digital read-out certainly look
elegant – but it is also extremely practical. Its quartz crystal move
ment keeps precision time! And the pen with its slim good looks wi
make writing a pleasure.

3. AN EXCITING MYSTERY BONUS – FREE!
And still your luck holds! You'll also receive a special mystery bonu
You'll be thrilled with this surprise gift. It will be the source of man
compliments as well as a useful and attractive addition to your hom

PLUS

**THERE'S MORE. THE DECK IS STACKED IN YOUR FAVOR. HER
ARE THREE MORE WINNING POINTS. YOU'LL ALSO RECEIVE**

4 . A MONTHLY NEWSLETTER – FREE!
It's "Heart to Heart" – the insider's privileged look at our most popul
writers, upcoming books and even recipes from your favorit
authors.

5 . CONVENIENT HOME DELIVERY
Imagine how you'll enjoy having the chance to preview the roma
tic adventures of our Harlequin heroines in the convenience of you
own home at less than retail prices! Here's how it works. Every mont
we'll deliver 8 new books right to your door. There's no obligation an
if you decide to keep them, they'll be yours for only $1.75! That's 20
less per book than what you pay in stores. And there's no extra charg
for shipping and handling.

6 . MORE GIFTS FROM TIME TO TIME – FREE!
It's easy to see why you have the winning hand. In addition to all th
other special deals available only to our home subscribers, you ca
look forward to additional free gifts throughout the year.

SO DEAL YOURSELF IN – YOU CAN'T HELP BUT WIN

write a "thank you" note to the children after dinner.'

'And what about me?'

She put her head to one side. 'I could write you a note, too.'

'A waste of paper.'

'I could say "Thank you, Graham, for the beautiful rose".'

'Actions speak louder than words. A well-known historical fact.'

She looked at him through her lashes. 'You mean I should show my appreciation by putting the roses in water?'

He leaned against the doorframe. He was wearing blue cords and a blue wool sweater over an open-necked shirt, and looked relaxed and at ease. 'For the sake of the roses, you should certainly do that. But for my sake . . .' He closed his eyes and puckered his lips.

'Oh!' she said, with the air of one making a great discovery. 'You want me to kiss you!'

'That was the general idea.'

His eyes were still closed. She stepped closer, pecked at his cheek and would have stepped back. But somehow his arm had snaked around her waist. 'You call that a kiss?'

'You didn't specify its nature or its duration.'

'I'd be arrested for obscenity. Put the roses down on the table, Jenny.'

'The masterful male,' she murmured.

'A role I frequently aspire to in your presence. Then put your arms around my neck.' Obediently she did as she was told, a move that brought her body delightfully close to his. 'Close your eyes. Now this is the kind of kiss that would show a proper degree of appreciation for a rose that not only smells good and has pretty red petals but also has more than its share of thorns; I shed blood for that rose!' And he bent his head and kissed her.

The kiss might have begun as a joke; it did not end as

one. When Graham raised his head, after a considerable length of time, Jenny was trembling, and aching with desire. She heard him say, 'I should have brought a dozen roses.'

'No, you shouldn't,' she retorted shakily. 'You'd be here till morning—think of the neighbours.'

'And the dinner!'

'Oh no—the sauce!' She pulled herself free and ran for the kitchen, Graham picking up the flowers and following at a more leisurely pace.

The sauce, delicately flavoured with shrimp and green onions, was poured over sole poached in white wine, and the whole concoction broiled to a golden brown; Jenny also served baked squash and slivered green beans, all on her best china. She put the roses on the table and lit the candles while Graham poured the wine. Suddenly nervous, she said shyly, 'I hope you'll like everything.'

'It looks delicious, Jenny.'

'I don't think of cooking as my strong point,' she confessed. 'But occasionally, when inspired, I surprise myself.'

'Am I to interpret that I was a source of inspiration?'

She chuckled. 'Oh, at least.' She felt wonderfully light-hearted. Graham looked very much at home, and she sensed he must be comfortable in her presence in order to show his streak of self-mockery. They bantered back and forth, talked more seriously about their philosophy of education and the role of the university in the community, and eventually left the table and moved to the living room with coffee and liqueurs.

Without fuss Jenny sat at the piano, and Graham moved to a chair where he could watch her face. She began with the brilliant Polonaise in A flat, then played her favourite waltz, followed by three of the Etudes. Then, reflectively, she drifted into the Nocturnes, losing herself in them as always. She had played perhaps six or seven before she glanced over at her audience.

He had leaned his head back and closed his eyes and for a moment she thought he was asleep: every performer's nightmare. But as her fingers slowed, his lashes flickered open.

'Getting tired?' he asked.

Automatically she continued to play. 'Not at all. I'd better warn you, I can play for hours!'

He sat forward in the chair. 'Because you love playing.'

'You're stating the obvious—of course I do.'

'No of course about it. By the end of his life my father hated playing. When he practised it was like a battle between him and the piano. He fought it, cursed it, tried to impose his will on it, and was ultimately defeated by it. But I don't know that he ever loved it.'

'Gillie would never be like that,' said Jenny with absolute conviction.

'Gillie's only seven. How can you tell?'

'Intuition—and don't tell me that's a typically female response!'

He smiled. 'I made a resolve before I came here tonight that we weren't going to talk about the children. Night off. Do you like to dance, Jenny?'

'Love to.'

'Got any dance music?'

She rooted among her record collection while Graham moved the living-room furniture back against the wall. They began with waltzes and foxtrots and a degree of dignity, moved to jives and calypso, and collapsed breathless.

'That was fun!' Jenny gurgled, laughing across at her companion, yet knowing that in one sense she was telling only part of the truth. The dancing *had* been fun, and had shown her a new and delightful side to Graham's personality. But it had also involved a lot of touching: fleeting contacts charged with—for her at least—a wanton and heady excitement. Had Graham felt the same excitement? Or had he simply been having fun without entertaining any thoughts about taking her to bed?

One of her first impressions of him had been his sense of ease with his own body; he had danced without self-consciousness and with total enjoyment. Would he make love the same way? she wondered. And will I ever find out?

She was not to find out that evening. He left shortly afterwards, kissing her once, swiftly, at the door. She went to bed, trying to ignore an ache of disappointment, planning to lie awake and go over every detail of the evening, and fell asleep while remembering the different colours of the roses.

At three o'clock the next afternoon Jenny's office phone rang. She picked up the receiver. 'Jenny Sprague.'

'Graham Tyson.'

She giggled. 'Hello, Graham Tyson.'

'Hello, Jenny Sprague. I'm calling to ask you for a date.'

'Good heavens—number three!'

'Go home and get your swimsuit and grab a bite to eat—I'll pick you up in an hour. We're going to the beach.'

'You're supposed to say, "Jenny, would you like to go to the beach"?'

'I'm out of practice. I trust Max doesn't have a prior claim?'

Max always called several days in advance and planned things very carefully. 'He doesn't, no.'

'Good. I'd hate to have to beat him up! See you in an hour.' And he rang off.

Jenny smiled foolishly at the rose bushes and shut her book. An analysis of the late Beethoven sonatas could wait until tomorrow.

When Graham came for her she was sitting on the front steps waiting for him, chewing an apple. She had a cotton cover-up over her bikini and a towel slung over her shoulder. As he got out of the car and walked towards her, she saw he was wearing shorts and a tank top. 'You have nice legs,' she said amiably.

He gave a snort of laughter. 'So do you. What about the rest of me?'

She let her eyes wander over his torso. 'The rest's okay, too.'

'If you took off that white thing, I'd be in a much better position to return the compliment On the other hand, if you take it off we may never get to the beach.'

She fluttered her lashes. 'Promise?'

He reached down and hauled her to her feet. 'I said I was taking you to the beach and so I am.'

'A man of determination! Which beach?'

'You'll see.'

'Aren't the children with you?'

'Nope. Jason is home, Gillie's having supper with a friend—she wasn't feeling that well this afternoon, I hope she's all right to go out—and Daniel has a soccer game ... Don't tell me you made those on-coming remarks a few minutes ago because you thought you were safe?'

'I'll never tell,' Jenny rejoined primly, and opened the car door.

They drove to the Northumberland Strait, then bumped along a maze of dirt roads until Graham pulled up by an old apple tree at the edge of a field where a herd of Holsteins gazed at them in stolid wonder. Beyond the field the sea sparkled in the sun, breakers rolling on to a pale curve of sand. Except for the gulls, the beach was deserted.

'What a beautiful spot,' Jenny said. 'But don't leave me here, will you, I'd never find my way back.'

His eyes were warm. 'I have no intentions of leaving you here.'

Unaccountably she found herself blushing. 'Let's swim,' she said hurriedly.

For nearly an hour they dived and splashed and played in the boisterous rollers, and all the while, unacknowledged, sexual tension crackled between them. They ran out of the water to their heap of discarded clothing. Picking up her towel, Jenny began to dry herself off.

Graham was watching her. Her hands stilled, the damp towel brushing her thighs. Droplets of water were trickling down his chest and legs, while his body hair was sleeked, seal-like, to his skin. Behind him the waves crashed to the sand and the sun blazed in the sky; she was very much aware of their solitude.

It was as if he had read her mind. 'This place is like Paradise, isn't it? Another Eden. And you and I alone in it.'

He took two steps towards her; she stumbled to meet him. Locked in his embrace, clinging to his wet body like a creature of the sea, she knew they might as well be naked and that paradise was to be in his arms.

He pulled her down on the sand. Dimly aware of its warm grittiness on her back, she exulted in his weight, in the dart of his tongue, in the hard thrust of his body between her legs. She opened her thighs, curling her legs around him and shamelessly rubbing her breasts against the dark pelt on his chest. They had not spoken a word to each other; their language was in the harshness of breath, the hot throbbing of blood, and the desperate, searching fingers.

She took his buttocks in her palms, feeling their clench as he sought to drive within her. His hand was tugging at the string on her bikini; she made a sound deep in her throat indicative of consent and longing and a fierce impatience.

His eyes opened. She looked into their agonised blue depths and knew that more than anything else in the world she wanted to replace that agony with the peace of fulfilment; the gift of paradise itself.

The hand which had been tugging at her bikini suddenly lay flat against her hip. He pushed himself up on one elbow. His head dropped.

His hair was cluster of wet, dark curls; one shoulder was coated with sand. 'Graham?' she whispered. 'Graham, what's the matter?'

'We mustn't make love—we must *not*,' he groaned. 'It would be all wrong.'

Something in his voice told her it was useless to argue. Yet she said, flatly, 'It doesn't feel wrong.'

'It feels as close to paradise as I've ever been,' he answered harshly. 'But it's still wrong.'

He rolled off her, looking down at his body as if he were not quite sure to whom it belonged. Then he stood up. Without looking at her he muttered, 'I'm going to wash the sand off.' Turning his back, he ran towards the sea and flung himself into the foam-white waves.

Jenny sat up. Paradise had vanished. The sea wind felt chill on her flesh, and the beach unbearably lonely. She spread her towel on the sand, flopped down on it, and buried her face in the crook of her elbow.

As the sun slowly warmed her back, the rhythm of the waves soothed her lacerated spirit. When Graham came padding up the beach ten minutes later she was asleep.

Jenny woke to feel hot, steamy breath blowing into her ear. Opening her eyes with a jerk, she saw a pair of pink rubbery lips stained with grass; big brown eyes fringed by incredibly long lashes were regarding her soulfully. She gave a yelp of dismay and sat up.

She and Graham were surrounded by cows. Huge black and white cows with swinging tails and twitching ears and bad breath. 'Graham,' she said, very loudly, 'I think we'd better find a farmer.'

He mumbled something and burrowed his head a little deeper in his arm; he was lying a discreet distance away from her. The biggest of the cows suddenly raised her head and emitted a long, mournful *moo*, whereupon Graham sat up as if he had been shot. 'Good God! Why didn't you wake me up? Where did they come from?'

He was grinning over at her as if he had never run away from her to throw himself in the cold breakers, and she was suddenly grateful that the cows had escaped from the pasture. 'The field, I would suspect,' she said.

'The question is, how do we get them back in the field? Do you want to stay here while I go in search of their owner?'

'I do not.'

'Coward—I thought you grew up on a farm.'

'A wheat farm, not a dairy farm.'

'The keys are in the car. I'll find a stick and see how many of them I can round up.' As he got to his feet, the two nearest cows wheeled and galumphed up the bank, udders swaying from side to side.

Jenny chuckled and risked saying, 'When I woke up, I thought it was *you* breathing into my shell-like ear!'

'Another time I'll be glad to oblige,' he responded easily. 'Go and find a farmer, Jenny.'

The farmer, a young man in a peaked cap, was located on a tractor a short distance down the road. He swore without animus when Jenny told him about the cows, abandoned the tractor, and went back with her in the car. Graham, still in his swimming trunks, had all six cows herded by the break in the fence; an active five minutes later the cows were back in the field and the farmer was stooping to mend the broken wire. They then drove him back to his tractor. He touched his cap, thanked them laconically, and climbed back on board.

Jenny said to Graham, 'Dates with you are not dull!'

'I aim to please.' He glanced over at her and added quietly, 'Do I please you, Jenny?'

'Oh yes , she whispered, 'you please me.'

He took her hand in his, raised it to his lips, then replaced it in her lap. She said at random, 'The children would have enjoyed the cows.'

'Jason would have told them where to go!'

'They probably would have obeyed—I foresee a long and interesting life ahead for Jason. For all your children, come to that. Gillie and her piano, and practical, down-to-earth Daniel. The Daniels of this world can move mountains.'

Graham gave her a keen sideways glance. 'You're fond of the children, aren't you?'

Jenny nodded, a smile still on her lips as she imagined Jason's strong will colliding with the barrel-like bulk of a pregnant Holstein. 'They're lovely children. You're very fortunate.'

'Would you be as interested in me if I didn't have them?' Graham asked lightly.

Her eyes lost their warmth. 'That's one of those questions that's impossible to answer, as well you know—so I won't try. How long have you had this car, Graham? Have you been pleased with it?'

His lips compressed, and for a moment she thought he was going to persist with his question. But then he said, 'Three years,' and for the rest of the journey they talked about petrol mileage and car prices rather than children.

However, the children were soon to make their presence known. As Jenny was opening the door to her house, Graham at her heels, the first thing she heard was the jangle of the telephone. She grabbed the receiver. 'Hello?'

A young boy's voice said, 'May I speak to Dr Tyson, please?'

'One moment . . . Graham, it's for you.'

He grimaced as he crossed the room. 'Gillie, I bet, I know she wasn't feeling well . . . hello.' A long pause, then he said, 'Okay, I'll be home as soon as I can. Tell Gillie I'm on the way. Thanks, Brian.' He put down the receiver. 'I'm sorry, Jenny, I've got to go home. It's not just Gillie. Jason is crying and Daniel is sick as well. Is there anything worse than a kid with stomach 'flu? I'm truly sorry—I hate rushing off like this.'

'If the three of them are ill, you'd better let me come with you.'

'Lord, no, I can manage.'

'Graham, you're a very capable man, but even you can't handle three sick children at once!'

'They're my responsibility,' he said stubbornly, and leaned forward to kiss her goodbye.

She evaded him, her eyes an angry blue. 'I'm offering to help, Graham, it wouldn't hurt you to accept.'

'I don't need any help.'

'There are times when everyone needs help. And this, for you, is one of them.'

'Jenny, I haven't got time to argue——'

'Good. I'll go and put a skirt on.'

More loudly he said, 'There's no need——'

'That's it,' she said with dangerous calm. 'You used that word "need" again. Do you know what your problem is, Graham? You can't say "I need you". You're determined to do everything on your own just to prove what a fabulous father you are. I know what a fabulous father you are—you don't need to prove it to me. Three of your kids are sick and I'm offering to help hold their heads or change their pyjamas or whatever needs doing. So stop pretending you're omnipotent and that you don't need help. Say it, Graham—say, "Jenny, I could use your help for a couple of hours". I bet you fifty dollars the sky won't fall!'

He looked dazed. As she paused for breath, he said

meekly, 'Jenny, I could use——'

'You're too proud to even—*what* did you say?'

'Jenny, I could use your help for a couple of hours.'

'Oh!' Her jaw dropped. 'Really?'

'If the offer still stands.'

'Oh, yes!'

'Were you expecting me to rant and roar and storm out of the house?'

'I wasn't expecting you to give in so easily.'

'You're very persuasive when you lose your cool.' As she blushed, he added patiently, 'Can we go now?'

'Oh! Oh, yes! Just let me put on a skirt and get my bag. I'd better take my own car so you don't have to drive me home. I won't be a minute.'

'I'll wait outside.'

A few minutes later she was driving behind him into town. She should have been feeling ashamed of herself for losing her temper so thoroughly, but she was not. The words had needed saying, and Graham had listened.

Lights were shining upstairs and down in the big grey and white house. Jenny parked on the side of the road and ran up the steps behind Graham. As soon as he opened the door she heard Jason crying, a full-bodied bellow that resounded down the stairwell. 'He's frightened, not hurt,' Graham said instantly. 'You get so you can tell the difference.' He flung his wet towel over the banister and they hurried upstairs.

Gillie was in the bathroom, sitting on the edge of the tub, her face as white as the porcelain sink. Daniel was huddled on top of his bed holding his stomach and moaning. Jason, scarlet-faced in the arms of the hapless Brian, went from forte to fortissimo when he saw his father, and lunged towards him, chubby arms outstretched.

'I'll look after Gillie,' said Jenny.

As it turned out, she looked after Gillie and Jason

upstairs while Graham coped with Daniel and the washer and drier downstairs. The stomach 'flu was of a particularly tenacious type. By one o'clock in the morning Jason had dark circles under his eyes but wanted nothing to do with his crib, while Gillie was clinging to Jenny as if she were her long-lost mother. So Jenny climbed into bed with her, cuddling the little girl into her left arm, and persuaded Jason to lie on her other side. She pulled the covers up over them and very softly began to sing. Her repertoire of lullabies was not large, but it was enough. Jason started to snore, long bubbling sighs from his pink lips; he looked like a plump, adorable cherub, Jenny decided, secretly delighting in the warmth and weight of him against her side. Gillie, in constrast, felt as frail as thistledown, her breathing shallow, blue shadows under her eyes.

The bedroom was in semi-darkness. The wallpaper had all the Beatrix Potter characters, prickly Mrs Tiggywinkle, prim Jemima Puddleduck with her yellow bill, Peter Rabbit in his blue jacket, clutching a carrot: images of Jenny's own childhood. She lay still, listening to the children breathe on either side of her, feeling safe and warm in the old-fashioned, comfortable bed. If she had her own children it would be like this, she decided, the thought bringing with it a strange contentment rather than the usual pain. Gillie's teddy bear smiled at her benignly from the foot of the bed. He was missing an eye. She should sew it on . . . her eyes closed and her own breathing deepened.

Half an hour later Graham came upstairs carrying Daniel. In broad daylight Daniel would have been too mindful of his position as the eldest to allow himself to be carried, but in the small hours of the morning he was content to have his arms looped around Graham's neck and his head on his father's shoulder. Graham tucked him in bed and kissed him good night just as the grandfather clock in the living room chimed twice.

The house was very quiet. He went out into the hall. 'Jenny?' he murmured in a low voice. She did not answer.

He did not think she would have left without telling him. Walking over to Gillie's room, he put his head around the door.

He saw the three occupants of the bed immediately. Gillie was sprawled across Jenny's stomach, while Jason's dark curls lay against her breast. Jenny, flat on her back, was sound asleep. She was fully dressed; her hair, spread on the pillow, was curly where Gillie's was straight, with the warmth of the sun rather than the pallor of the moon.

Very carefully Graham sat down at the foot of the bed beside the teddy bear, feeling desire gnaw at his vitals. *His* head should be where Jason's was, *his* fingers tangled in Jenny's hair like Gillie's. But if it were so, he would not want her to be asleep . . .

Downstairs the clock signalled the quarter hour. He should wake Jenny up and send her home. Mrs Magnusson across the street would already have noticed her car and drawn all the most obvious conclusions. The worst part about them, thought Graham wryly, getting to his feet, is that they would be untrue.

He did not have the heart to disturb Jenny. She had worked like a Trojan until well into the morning, and, like him, she had classes and students to face in a matter of a few hours. He bent over, brushed his lips against hers, and left the room.

CHAPTER SEVEN

WHEN Jenny woke up she thought she was dreaming. There was a weight across one arm, a warm, breathing weight, and on her opposite side an elbow shoved into her ribs. The Flopsy Bunnies smiled at her from the wall. She seemed to be fully dressed.

In the dim light filtering through the red curtains she distinguished the weight as Jason's and the elbow as Gillie's and memory came rushing back. The children had been sick. She had yelled at Graham and followed him here and fallen asleep in his daughter's bed. I wish it had been his bed, she thought drowsily, then suddenly realised the significance of the chinks of light between the long red curtains. My God, she thought, it's morning! I've got a nine-thirty lecture!

She eased her arm from under Jason's head, feeling pins and needles tingle in her fingers. He mumbled something that sounded like no, no, no, then mercifully subsided into sleep again. In a very gingerly fashion Jenny sat up. She had no idea of the time. What if she'd overslept? How would she face her students? Or—worse—Dr Moorhead? 'Pardon me, sir, I spent the night at Dr Tyson's and forgot to set the alarm'. It would almost be worth it to see his face. Almost.

She stood up and shook out her skirt, which not surprisingly looked as if it had been slept in. A yawn caught her unawares. Maybe it was only early. Six o'clock. Maybe she could go back to bed . . . she yawned again and headed for the bathroom.

The door was ajar. Rubbing her eyes, she shoved it open with her bare toe and walked in. She saw Graham's face reflected in the mirror over the basin before she saw the rest of him. He had been shaving. He was wearing a pair of blue briefs and a few blobs of shaving cream, and nothing else.

'I'm sorry!' she gasped, beginning to back out of the room. 'I didn't know you were up! I——'

'It's okay,' he said easily, leaning over the basin to splash water on his face. 'Did you sleep well?'

She dragged her eyes away from the long curve of his spine in the smoothly muscled back. 'Yes. Thank you. Did you?'

'Sure did.' His voice was muffled by the towel. 'The problem will be to stay awake today!'

She was still standing, transfixed, by the door. He put the towel neatly over the rack and walked over to her. 'Good morning, Jenny.'

A triangle of dark hair covered his chest, its apex at his navel. The blue briefs were definitely brief. You're not seeing anything you didn't see at the beach, so keep your cool, Jenny, she thought. 'I must look a fright,' she muttered, pushing her tangled hair back from her face.

'You look sleep-warm and soft and very beautiful. And if I didn't have any children and if we didn't have lectures and students and meetings, I'd take you back to bed.'

She widened her eyes. 'Because you're still sleepy?'

He cupped her face in his palms. 'So I could make love to you.'

Her smile was pure mischief. 'Thank goodness!' she said. 'I was afraid I was the only one whose mind was on such lascivious matters.'

'You never have to worry about that when I'm with you,' he drawled, and touched his lips to hers. 'So right now you'd go to bed with me, would you, Jenny?'

'A rhetorical question,' she murmured, bringing her hands to his shoulders and feeling beneath her palms the smooth interplay of bone and muscle. 'Because any or all of the children could wake up at any minute and I do have a nine-thirty lecture.'

'Pretend the children are with their grandparents in Ontario and it's Saturday. Would you, Jenny?'

She dropped her eyes to her index finger, which was smoothing the hard curve of his collarbone. 'Yes, I would,' she said. 'You know that.'

'Why, Jenny? Why me and not Max?'

She looked up, her blue eyes troubled. 'It's partly because you're real in a way Max isn't—you have responsibilities and commitments, you love your children; I respect you so much for the way you handle everything. That part I can explain. The rest I can't.' Again her fingers traced the arc of bone. 'When I touch you like this my knees turn to jelly and my heart does all manner of peculiar things, and I wouldn't dare describe my thoughts to you.' She managed a smile. 'I can't explain why—can you?'

Graham kissed her with lips and tongue; as his hands moved to stroke the fullness of her breasts, he pressed his hips to hers and whispered against her mouth, 'How do you explain *that*?'

She put her arms around his waist and drew him closer. They kissed, passionately, for several minutes. Then Jenny pulled free. 'Graham, stop—because we can't!'

The pulse was pounding at the base of his throat. 'You're right, we can't,' he said hoarsely. 'This is madness—sheer madness. You know that as well as I do, don't you? There are a million reasons to keep us out of that bed.'

'Only three,' she answered, trying to tuck her blouse back into her waistband. 'Their names are Daniel, Gillie and Jason.'

He drew a long, shuddering breath. 'It's not that simple, Jenny. The children really like you. Gillie and Daniel would have put a curse on Max if they could! No, it's more than the children.' Deliberately he moved away from her and added with seeming irrelevance, 'Your car was parked on the street all night. The neighbour across the road, who has binoculars for eyes and a video recorder for a brain, will have taken note of that fact and will no doubt take note of your departure as well. Unfortunately she will also see fit to broadcast it—confidentially, of course.'

Jenny said bluntly, 'You mean it will be all over town that I spent the night with you?' As he nodded, she added in exasperation, 'I can't believe people are that interested!'

'Brockton's a small town and the winters are long— what else is there to talk about? Mrs Layton will be arriving in a few minutes, too, but she's no problem. If I tell her you stayed to help out with the children she'll believe me. No, it's Elva Magnusson I worry about.'

'We don't have to pay any attention to gossip. *We* know the truth.'

'She's one of the reasons I shut myself off from help, Jenny—because you were right, you know, last night. After Mona died Elva and her ilk would come over here and tell the children what poor little things they were now that they didn't have a mother, and at the same time they'd be running their fingers over the furniture to see how the dust was collecting and checking the refrigerator to see what we were having for supper.'

'Curiosity divorced from caring.'

'Yeah . . . there were those who cared, don't get me wrong. But one has to stand on one's own two feet.'

'Which is not to say someone can't stand beside you.'

Some of the tension eased from his face. 'You have an answer for everything, Jenny.'

'Not quite everything,' she said drily. 'What's the time, Graham?'

'Five past eight.'

'I must go home and change.' She looked down at herself. 'The students are broad-minded as far as clothes are concerned, but this would be pushing it.'

'Will you do me a favour?'

'Of course,' she said without hesitation.

'Drop in here a little after five?'

'Well, yes ... but why?'

'That's the second part of the favour—you're not to ask why.'

'By far the more difficult part!'

'I figured it would be. Wait a second while I throw on some clothes—I don't want you to face Mrs Layton on your own.'

Jenny closed the door behind him and attempted to make herself a little more respectable; Mrs Layton and Mrs Magnusson seemed a formidable pair to face without benefit of toothbrush or clean clothes. Generous dollops of *L'Air du Temps* helped her confidence, if not her appearance.

She trailed down the stairs behind Graham and followed him into the kitchen, where he said casually, 'Coffee, Jenny? Jenny stayed to help me with the children, Muriel, all of them are down with stomach 'flu.'

'I thought Gillie looked peaked yesterday. Morning, Miss Sprague, dear. Coffee's on the stove.' And Muriel Layton went back to scouring the sink as unconcerned as if Graham brought a woman downstairs with him every morning.

'Thank you, Mrs Layton. But I'd better go straight home,' Jenny said hurriedly. 'I have to change and pick up my notes.'

'Okay,' Graham said. 'I'll see you to your car.

They went out the back door and round the side of the house. The sun was shining, the sky a pale, pristine blue. In the garden across the street a plump, red-haired woman was busily pruning the rose bushes, of which there were many. 'Mrs Magnusson,' said Graham in a low voice. 'Damnation! I was hoping *she* might have had stomach 'flu! She was at your recital, so she'll know who you are—I hate the thought of her gossiping about you, Jenny.'

He looked genuinely angry. Jenny, who had been inclined to think he was exaggerating the dangers of Elva Magnusson, began to realise that he was not. '*We* know the truth,' she repeated stoutly. 'That's what counts.' She took her keys out of her purse and smiled up at him. 'After all, she couldn't have seen me lusting after you in the bathroom.'

'A two-way lust, my dear.'

'I was given a hint to that effect!'

He suddenly gripped her by the arm; across the street the pruning stilled. 'I *do* need you, Jenny,' he said huskily. 'I need your sense of fun and your generosity. Thank you for staying last night.'

Gravely she held out her hand. 'Any time,' she said.

'Five o'clock today will do for a start.' He shook her hand, said, 'To hell with Elva Magnusson,' and kissed her on the mouth. Quickly Jenny got in the car and drove home.

Nine hours later, when Jenny parked the car in the identical spot on the road, she noticed the net curtains twitch in the front windows of Elva Magnusson's green-painted Victorian house. It had been a long day. She contemplated waving, then thought the better of it.

Graham let her in, kissing her as if the nine hours had been as long for him as they had been for her. Someone giggled behind the kitchen door.

Graham scowled. 'Gillie?'

The little girl who poked her head around the door looked very different from the pathetic, shivering child who had sat on the edge of the bathtub at one a.m. 'I just won a dime!' she crowed. 'Daniel didn't think you'd kiss her and I did.'

'Kissing's dumb,' said Daniel in disgust, also appearing.

'The time will come when you'll change your mind,' his father commented. 'Where's Jason?'

'Asleep,' Gillie said.

'You've all recovered!' exclaimed Jenny, amazed.

'We stayed home from school,' Daniel announced complacently.

'Listen, Daniel,' Graham interjected, 'Jenny and I have something to discuss with Gillie in the den. Vamoose for five or ten minutes, will you? Then we'll have supper.'

As Daniel obediently headed for the door, Gillie said, 'What are we going to talk about?' a question Jenny also felt like asking.

'You'll see. Come along.'

They went into the den, which seemed to contain more piles of books than the last time. Graham closed the door. 'Gillie,' he said without preamble, 'do you still want to have piano lessons with Jenny?'

The child looked from one to the other of them. 'Oh, yes! Yes, I do!'

'She's more than willing to teach you. And I've come to understand how wrong I've been to deprive you of lessons.'

'You mean I can have lessons? Every week? With Jenny?' With each question Gillie's voice went up a notch, and to each question Graham nodded in response.

She clasped her hands to her breast and burst into tears.

'Gillie, dear——' Graham began, appalled.

'It's 'cause I'm so happy!' the child sobbed. 'I wanted lessons so much! Oh, Jenny . . .' And she flung her arms around Jenny's waist and wept into her blouse as if her heart was breaking.

Jenny rocked her back and forth and looked over at

Graham. In the conflicting emotions in his face, remorse predominated. His hands were deep in his pockets; his eyes were wet. She said very softly, 'Thank you, Graham.'

Gillie lifted her tear-streaked face. 'I'll pay you every cent of my allowance, Jenny.'

'You don't have to do that,' Jenny replied. 'Your father will pay for the lessons. But you can pay me by practising every day, by learning as much as I can teach you, and by expressing your love of music for all to hear.'

'That's easy,' Gillie said, puzzled.

'You don't know what a slave driver I can be,' Jenny joked. 'Have you got a handkerchief?'

Gillie pulled a ragged tissue from the pocket of her jeans and scrubbed her face. 'When can we start?'

'Let me think for a minute . . . I want the lessons at my place, on my piano. Saturday morning or Wednesday evening . . . Wednesday's an easy day at work. I could pick you up and bring you home.'

'We'll split that between us,' Graham interjected.

Not a tone of voice with which she would argue. Anyway, a naughty little voice whispered in her ear, that means you'll see him at least once a week. All winter. 'All right. Which day is better for you?'

'Wednesday, I think—Saturdays are usually chaos around here. Wednesday okay with you, Gillie?'

Midnight on Sunday would have been fine with Gillie. 'Sure. 'Cept I have to wait a whole week.' She looked up at Jenny hopefully.

'I think you will have to wait. None of us got much sleep last night. I can prepare some lesson plans in the meantime, too . . . I'm looking forward to teaching you, Gillie.'

The child's smile was brilliant. 'Thank you,' she said with the politeness that Graham had somehow managed to instil in both his older children.

But not in Jason, thought Jenny, hearing a familiar bellow penetrate the closed door. 'Does that mean he's hurt, or hungry, or merely signalling to the world that he's awake?' she asked.

'Hungry,' said Jason's father. 'As am I, although I've learned to be a little more restrained in expressing it. Stay and have supper with us, Jenny, there's lots—if you're free, that is?'

'I'd love to stay.'

As they ate Mrs Layton's delicious meat pie and creamy custard pudding, Jenny found herself watching the interactions between Graham and his children, and soon discovered that mealtimes in the Tyson household were not for gobbling food as quickly as possible; they were also a time for conversation. Graham talked to his children, but more importantly he listened to them, communication skills that the children were already picking up. Gillie's piano lessons, Daniel's high mark in his mathematics test and his low mark in English all came up for discussion, and Jenny was astute enough to realise that far more than a simple exchange of information was going on. Family ties were being preserved and strengthened, and a man who could only spend a limited number of hours a day with his children was keeping his finger on the pulse of their lives.

Clearing up afterwards was clearly a routine, for Gillie put away the food and washed the saucepans while Daniel loaded the dishwasher; Graham and Jenny took coffee into the living room and Jason got in everyone's way.

As Jenny sipped her coffee, a Java blend which was hot and very good, she felt long-familiar symptoms begin to nibble at her nerves. She had realised many years ago that she should not get over-tired, because when she was tired she was prey to black thoughts about her inability to have children. Now, as she watched Jason fling blocks at the fire-screen with amazing accuracy, she could easily recognise the lump in the pit of her stomach as envy. She envied Graham. His daily routine was hectic and the demands made upon him were many, but in this big, comfortable house he was surrounded by love. She thought of her own empty house, and ached at the contrast. She had a freedom that was completely out of Graham's reach, but she also suffered an isolation which he would never know.

She tried to swallow her coffee more quickly, suddenly desperate to leave the noise and confusion and happiness that overflowed in every room of this house. As her cup rattled against its saucer Graham asked, 'What's wrong, Jenny?'

'Oh, nothing. Tired, I guess.'

'You look unhappy.'

The cup was nearly empty. She said, a slight edge to her voice, 'I said I was tired, Graham.'

'So I'm to mind my own business—is that the message? I thought we'd progressed beyond that point.'

'Obviously not,' she snapped, knowing she was behaving atrociously but unable to stop.

He made one more effort, leaning forward in his chair. 'Please, Jenny, tell me why you looked so unhappy. Maybe I can help.'

If she had not been feeling so miserable, she might have laughed. 'You can't,' she said wildly, gulping the last of her coffee.

Jason fired his one remaining brick at the screen, smiled with satisfaction at the rattle it made and looked around for distraction. His deep blue eyes, so like his father's, fell on Jenny. He gave her a fat smile, as if he and she shared a marvellous joke that no one else knew about, and headed in her direction with single-minded speed.

With something akin to panic Jenny scrambled to her feet. She could not bear it if Jason threw himself into her arms; she would burst into tears just like Gillie, and then what would Graham think? With a blind little gesture she warded Jason off. 'I've got to go, tell Gillie I'll see her next Wednesday, I'll call her to arrange a time.' She went around the back of the chair, almost running, her eyes hunted.

Graham grabbed her sleeve. 'You can't leave like this——'

'I can do whatever I like!' she cried, even more wildly, and fought down a hysterical giggle at the total untruth of her words. That was the whole problem: she could not do the one thing in the world that should have been the most natural. 'Let go, Graham!'

'When am I going to see you again?'

'*I* don't know——'

'Did someone say something to you today—about you spending the night here?'

'No! That's got nothing to do with it. I'm sorry, Graham, I know I'm not making any sense to you, but I just want to go *home*.' In spite of her best intentions, her voice wobbled.

His face changed. He's going to stop me, she thought. And then I'll end up crying my eyes out and telling him everything. She ducked under his arm, grabbed her bag from the floor by the chesterfield and ran for the door.

She never even saw him move. But somehow he was between her and the door, his grip on her arm spinning her around. Her bag went flying, hit the chesterfield with a thud and spilled half its contents on the floor. '*Now* look what you've done!' Jenny cried, and did indeed burst into tears.

From a long way away she was aware of Graham pulling her against his chest so that her sobs were muffled in his shirt-front. The kitchen door squeaked open. She heard him speak to the children and heard Jason's wail of protest, then there was only the sound of someone weeping as if her heart would break—and that someone was herself.

Eventually she stopped. 'I need to wash my face,' she snuffled.

He kept his arm around her. 'Come on into the kitchen—the kids are out playing. I'm not letting you out of my sight until you've told me what this is all about.'

She could scarcely blame him, she supposed. At the kitchen sink she splashed quantities of cold water over her face, blew her nose, and became aware of a leaden, exhausted emptiness.

Graham put a rum and Coke in her hand and steered her back to the chesterfield. He sat down next to her. 'Give,' he said. 'It's something to do with the children, isn't it? And your broken engagement . . . why *didn't* you get married, Jenny?

She swirled the glass so the ice cubes chased each other round and round. 'Because I can't have children,' she said.

He took the glass from her fingers, put it on the table, and covered her hands witn his, chafing them to warm them. 'I don't understand.'

'When I was twenty I was very ill,' she said tonelessly. 'Something called endometriosis. I had to have a partial hysterectomy. I can never have children, Graham.'

The silence in the room was absolute and seemed to Jenny to last forever. Marc's peat-brown hair and tanned features swam across her vision; she saw Samuel's neatly trimmed beard and cool blue eyes. Then Graham said, 'Jenny, I'm so sorry——'

'Don't feel sorry for me! I can't stand that.'

He hesitated, choosing his words. 'I'm sorry because you're a warm, loving woman who should be able to hold your child to your breast.'

'It's partly my looks,' she said fiercely. 'I look so damned fecund, all curves and promise. That's what you mean, isn't it? But I'm a fake. My appearance is a lie. I can never be a whole woman.'

He let go of her hand, got up and pulled her to her feet. He was as angry as she had ever seen him. 'You *are* a whole woman!' he blazed. 'Don't give me that garbage, Jenny Sprague!'

'I'm not whole!' she cried. 'I can't have babies! Who'd ever want to marry me?'

She could almost see his brain making the connection. 'The man in New York ... what happened, Jenny?'

She was oblivious to the grip of his fingers on her arms; only the next day would she see the bruises. 'Not one man, Graham—two.' She laughed wildly. 'Two broken engagements in three years—not a bad record, huh?'

'Stop feeling so goddamned sorry for yourself and tell me what happened.'

She glowered at him. 'All right, I'll tell you. At the age of twenty-two I fell head over heels in love with Marc. He was—still is, I suppose—an advertising executive who was crazy about opera—that's where we met. I told him soon after we met that I couldn't have children. It didn't seem to matter, because he was crazy about me, too. We got engaged, we met his parents—stuffy, upper-crust New Yorkers—we set the wedding date. His father had been making noises about carrying on the family line, Marc Foster III and all that, but I hadn't really paid much attention. A week before the wedding Marc decided he couldn't marry me, he wanted to have children and adoption wouldn't do, there was the family name to consider, the bloodline, etcetera, etcetera.' Her breath caught in a hiccup. 'I was stunned. When the shock wore off, I was like a—a creature that's been stripped of its skin, of its protective outer covering. Raw, vulnerable, in pain ... Well, a few months later I met Samuel. He was a bassoonist with the New York Philharmonic. Dark, detached, hated Verdi ... the antithesis of Marc. And he didn't want children—ever.

He made that quite clear. Inevitable, I suppose, that I should convince myself I was in love with him. The word is rebound. Anyway, we decided to get married, a very small wedding, none of the splash and social furore that a Foster wedding would have meant. But I wasn't so overwrought that I didn't bring up the subject of adopting a child. Although I knew I couldn't have my own, I didn't want to close off the possibility of being a mother in some form. Samuel was . . .' she gave a faint, reminiscent smile that did not reach her eyes, '. . . affronted. In my experience bassoonists seem to cultivate a high degree of dignity, it must go with the instrument. Also, which was not so amusing, he was adamant. No children, his or anyone else's. A Siamese cat maybe, but not a child. So, just for variety, I broke off the engagement. To be honest, I think he was relieved.'

'He sounds like a cold stick to me.'

'That's as good a description as any.'

'Are you still in love with either of them?'

'No. It took a long time to get over Marc—he was the first, and only, man I've ever slept with. I don't think I was really in love with Samuel, I just told myself I was. Because he didn't want children.'

'Jenny, I'm going to repeat myself,' Graham said soberly. 'I'm sorry. You've had to do one hell of a lot of growing up in the last five years, haven't you? The operation, the limitations of your career and then two unhappy love affairs. Neither man used you well— Marc worse than Samuel, I'd say, because Samuel was at least straightforward. Marc let you think everything was lovely in the garden until the very last minute.'

Restlessly Jenny pulled her hands free. 'You can hardly blame him, it's natural enough for a man to want to father a child. After all, who'd want to marry a woman who can't have children?'

'Quite a few people, I would think. Someone who's in the same position as I am, for instance.'

Jenny hugged her arms across her breast. 'What do you mean?'

'I already have three children, right? Why would I want more? All I'm trying to say, Jenny, is that there are a lot of men out there with young children who'd be delighted to marry you . . . But that's beside the point. What really bothers me is that you don't see yourself as a whole person, that you've allied your worth as a woman to your inability to bear a child—that's nonsense, you know. Total nonsense. You're a warm, generous, loving woman. You're doing yourself a terrible disservice if you see yourself as less than whole.'

He was speaking with passionate intensity, and she knew he believed every word he was saying. 'I see,' she said.

'*Do* you see? Do you believe me, Jenny?'

She tried to be as truthful as she could. 'My head tells me you're right. But emotionally I'm not sure I can accept what you're saying.'

'You're an intelligent, gifted and beautiful woman,' he said forcefully, 'who happens to be unable to have children. That's not irrelevant—but it's not of major importance, which is what you've made it.'

The exhaustion was rolling over her like sullen grey waves on a lonely shore, and she felt a sudden, desperate craving to be alone. 'Graham, I've got to go home,' she said. 'I'm worn out.'

'You'll think about what I've said?'

'Yes.'

A smile lightened the inflexibility of his features. 'Now I'll pick up the quite astonishing array of articles that came out of your handbag so you can take it home with you—is it always that full?'

Mrs Magnusson, if she was watching five minutes later, would have seen a blonde-haired woman with a bag over her shoulder walk heavily down the steps, get in her car and drive away without looking back. She would also have seen Graham Tyson standing in the doorway to watch the car until it had disappeared from sight.

The next morning Jenny bumped into Lois in the crowded corridors of the Music building. Lois gave her a sharp look. 'Are you free for lunch?'

'At twelve-thirty. Love your outfit!'

Lois was wearing an orange and black jumpsuit that must have raised Dr Moorhead's blood pressure. 'Oh, thanks,' Lois said, not even glancing down at herself. 'Come to my place right after class.'

Although Jenny was used to Lois's abrupt pronouncements, the invitation had seemed more than usually terse. But one of Jenny's piano students wanted to change his lesson time and she had a listening quiz to organise for her keyboard literature course, so any strangeness in Lois's behaviour was forgotten.

Lois greeted her with a glass of excellent dry sherry and said, as if they were continuing a conversation already in progress, 'I hear you've succumbed to the sexiest man on campus.'

Jenny helped herself to a handful of chips from the pottery bowl Lois was holding out. Damn Elva Magnusson and the pruning shears . . . 'Tell me what you heard,' she said.

Lois plunked the bowl back on the counter. 'You're crazy—you know that?'

Jenny had not slept well, and in her dreams had seen Graham and his children holding hands and dancing in a tight little circle from which she had been excluded. 'Why don't you tell me what this is all about?' she said evenly, for it did no good to rant and roar with Lois.

'I heard, via the grapevine, that you're sleeping with Graham Tyson.'

'You can tell the grapevine it got the story twisted.'

'You spent the night at his house.'

'That, certainly, is correct.'

'*Jenny!* It's Max you're dating!'

'I have had three genuine dates with Professor Tyson.'

'You've changed,' Lois said nastily. 'You never used to go to bed with anyone after three dates.'

'You're not listening to me, Lois. I did *not* go to bed with Graham Tyson—although I did sleep with two of his children.'

Lois's cheeks, pink with temper, clashed with her jumpsuit. 'Max is really interested in you, I know he is. He's exactly what you need.'

'Lois, my love, you should know by now that human emotions are not noted for their aura of common sense or rationality. I agree with you, Max would be a wonderful catch and I'm probably a fool not to be getting into bed with him. But I'm not. Because I don't want to.'

'So why didn't you get into Graham's?'

'A small matter of three very sick children. You should tell your particular tendril of the grapevine to check his or her facts. Stomach 'flu is something of a barrier to romance. Or lust.'

Lois took a tray of croissants topped with broiled crabmeat out of the oven. 'Graham Tyson has been quoted as saying he'll never remarry.'

Jenny tried to ignore the sinking feeling in the vicinity of her stomach. 'I trust that's as inaccurate as the report that he and I are sleeping together.'

Lois made it a statement rather than a question. 'You'd like to marry him. Come and eat while they're hot.'

Jenny might not always trust Lois's temper, but she did trust her discretion. 'I don't set my sights quite that high. But I would like to go to bed with him . . .' Then, because she was incurably honest, she added through a mouthful of flaky croissant and creamed crab, 'Who am

I trying to fool? If he did ask me to marry him, I can't imagine saying anything other than yes. Ridiculous when you think about it. I hardly know him.'

'And he has all those children . . .'

'Lois, you have to admit that all those children, as you so scathingly put it, would be an ideal solution for me.'

'You always did want children.' Lois could as well have been saying that Jenny had always wanted to be a prostitute.

Jenny winced. 'Yes,' she said steadily.

'Sorry, darling! I didn't mean to hurt you—I thought perhaps you'd changed.'

'Grown more accustomed to the fact that I won't have them, but scarcely changed. You never have understood why I want children so badly, have you? I suppose because you've never wanted them yourself.'

'I—no.'

'Lois—don't tell me you're the one who's changed!'

'Of course not,' Lois said with asperity. 'Except that I'm pushing thirty-two and Terry's thirty-seven next week, and if we're going to . . .'

Wistfulness sat oddly on Lois's forceful features. Intrigued, Jenny said, 'Is that why you've been so down on Graham's children, because you're determined not to show you might want one or two yourself? Lois, what a hypocrite you are!'

Lois gave a sudden grin. 'If you're shocked, imagine how Terry felt when I broached the subject!'

'Is he for it or against it?'

Lois helped herself to another croissant. 'Wanting to be talked out of being against it. I think.' She did not sound very sure of herself.

'If anyone can talk him into or out of anything, you can.'

'He says if we have kids, he won't be able to play his trumpet at midnight.'

'Get a soundproof door to their room.'

'I suggested a mute for the trumpet. Didn't go down very well.'

'You might hatch a brood of little virtuosos. Or is it virtuosi? Who'll cheer him on when he plays the trumpet at midnight.'

'I hadn't thought of that. Oh darn, Jenny, I don't know. Let's change the subject. What did you think of the latest memo the comptroller sent around?'

For the next half an hour they religiously discussed university matters. But when Jenny got up to leave she squeezed Lois's black-clad sleeve and said sincerely, 'Good luck with tne decision.'

Lois pouted her orange mouth. 'Can you see me in maternity clothes?'

'You'd be the most stylish expectant professor on campus,' said Jenny, touched by this new side to her tough, decisive friend.

Lois's shudder was only partly feigned. 'Like a big striped balloon . . . Jenny, next time you stay overnight with Graham Tyson, be sure it's him you sleep with, not his children.'

Jenny blushed. 'That was one chance in a lifetime, I'm sure,' she said. Which went to show how wrong she could be.

Jenny had an unexpected visitor later that afternoon: Max. She had run for three miles on the marshes and was just jogging the last few steps along her driveway when a car pulled in behind her. She leaned her palms against her own car to stretch out her leg muscles and called out, 'Hi, Max! This is a nice surprise.'

He slammed his car door. 'Can we go inside?'

Max, unlike Lois, was never abrupt. 'What's wrong?' she asked in a puzzled voice.

'I need to talk to you.'

She made a shrewd guess. 'And what have *you* heard?'

'So you know why I'm here—I wondered if you would.'

'I think I do. But——'

'Inside.'

She debated arguing with him, then decided it might be politic to do as he was suggesting; he looked very angry. Too angry, she thought. What had he heard?

She led the way into the house. 'Can I offer you a beer?'

'No, thanks. This isn't a social call.'

'Well, I need a glass of water. Excuse me a minute.'

In the kitchen she had a drink, splashed some water on her flushed face and decided to keep on her pink nylon shell; the T-shirt underneath showed too much cleavage for Max in his present mood. After running a comb through her hair, she went back into the living-room. Deciding to go on the attack, she said, 'I suppose you too have heard that I'm Graham Tyson's mistress?'

The anachronistic word hung in the air between them. His eyes narrowed. 'Yeah . . . that's exactly what I heard.'

I'd like to prune Elva Magnusson's tongue, Jenny thought viciously. 'You heard wrong.'

'Your car was parked outside his house all night. What were you doing—playing the piano?'

'Max, what's it to you? I told you now I felt about him, I thought you'd accepted that.'

'I thought I had, too. But I find I'm not as detached as I thought I was. On Saturday you turn me down. On Wednesday you sleep with him. How the devil do you think I feel about that?'

'By the look of you, quite angry.'

'Leave out the *quite*,' he snarled.

'Max, it's your pride that's hurt. Anyway, I didn't——'

'Damn right my pride is hurt.' He was pacing back and forth as he spoke. 'But it's not just my pride. I really care about you—I'm jealous as hell, if you want the truth!'

She was not sure she did, although she had it anyway. 'Max, listen to me!' she ordered. 'I stayed at Graham's house on Wednesday because all three children were ill and he couldn't cope on his own. I have not even been in his bedroom, let alone in his bed. But that's——'

Max interrupted her. 'You mean you didn't . . .' She could see him searching for a suitable euphemism.

'No, I didn't,' she said roundly. 'But if I'd been asked, I would have. So there's not much difference, is there?'

His mouth was grim. 'I was a fool not to haul you off to a hotel room on Saturday night.'

'I'd have belted you if you'd tried.'

Reluctantly he smiled. 'You probably would have . . . Jenny, are you sure you're interested in Graham? Maybe you just feel sorry for him.'

'I do not feel the slightest bit sorry for him. The chemistry's there. That's all I can say.'

'Will you be seeing him again?'

'I'm giving his daughter piano lessons, so I'll certainly be seeing him on a casual basis. As for the rest, I simply don't know.'

Max sat down heavily on the arm of the chesterfield. 'Maybe I will have that beer, after all,' he said.

Jenny went into the kitchen, wishing he would leave. Carrying the open beer bottle and a mug and wearing a smile, she went back into the living-room. 'Here you are.'

'Thanks.' He poured the beer down the slanted side of the mug. 'I've always prided myself on being detached. I have an affair and when I'm ready I move on to the next one. I don't allow myself to get emotionally involved and I never get coerced into any kind of commitment. I had no reason to believe I felt any differently about you. Except that ever since I was told about you and Graham I feel as though someone's slugged me over the head with a baseball bat.'

'I'm probably the first woman to say no to you.'

Some of the old carefree Max showed in his smile. 'True.'

'You're not used to that. Don't transform our friendship into a deathless love affair because it's unconsummated, Max.' She wrinkled her nose. 'Go on to the next one instead.'

In an injured tone of voice he said, 'You mean you want me to date someone else? Won't you even miss me?'

'I would miss you, yes. Maybe we can still see each other sometimes—as long as it's understood that I'm not coming across. Sorry to sound so crude, but that's the way it is.'

'Hands off.'

'That's right.'

He raised the beer mug and drained it, the muscles in his throat working. Jenny watched them, unmoved. Then he said, wiping the froth from his lips, 'You're a very beautiful woman.'

'Thank you,' she said as politely as if he were a stranger.

He put the mug on the carpet and stood up. 'Come on, Jenny—give me a kiss for old times' sake.'

She could scurry round the piano like a frightened rabbit or she could hold her ground. She chose the latter. 'Max, I think you should go.'

'I am going. After I kiss you.'

She compressed her lips and stood like a stick while he put his arms around her. Technically, no doubt, his kiss was more skilful than Graham's, but it left her blood cold and her heart untouched, and she was not at all surprised when Max thrust her away and said disgustedly, 'Dammit, Jenny, is that the best you can do?'

She was not going to apologise. 'Yes,' she said, her eyes defiant.

He hunched his shoulders. 'So that's the way it is . . . okay. Look, I know we had a date for tomorrow night, but I want out—the way I feel right now, I don't want to see you for a while.'

'No bed, no relationship,' she said, wondering why she should be hurt.

'That's not——'

'Yes, it is.'

'All right, so it is! I don't feel like genteel handshakes and nice little kisses on the cheek when I'm around you—why should I pretend otherwise? And don't say it, Jenny, I know I'm behaving like a spoiled kid . . . tell you what, in two weeks we'll have lunch together and compare notes. If neither of us has got to first base— well, we could always try again.'

'Nine innings in a baseball game?' Jenny queried wryly. 'Okay. Lunch in two weeks and good luck to both of us.'

'I'm not going to wish you good luck—I'm not that unselfish.' He gave her a quick hug to which she could not object, kissed her on both cheeks, winked and left. With a sigh Jenny sat down on the chesterfield. 'Men!' she said out loud to the empty room.

CHAPTER EIGHT

IF Jenny had hoped Graham would phone and suggest a date for the weekend, she was to be disappointed. Nobody phoned. Not even Dr Moorhead to fussily discuss some matter vital to the smooth functioning of the Music Department. Jenny could have picked up the phone herself. But Lois and Terry were no doubt involved in the Great Maternity Debate, in which Jenny did not wish to interfere or participate. She had nothing new to say to Max and her pride forbade her from calling Graham. So she went to the local library on Friday evening and loaded up with paperback mysteries, and rented a V.C.R. for the weekend together with three movies. She read well into the night on Friday, so was asleep when the telephone beside her bed did finally ring on Saturday morning. Wondering muzzily if this was all part of a dream, she croaked into the receiver, 'Hello?'

'Jenny? Is that you?'

'Yes, it's me. How are you, Gillie? Isn't it awfully early?'

'Not really,' Gillie said severely. 'It's eight o'clock. Daniel wanted me to call you sooner, but I thought I'd better wait. Dad's sick.'

Jenny gripped the receiver. 'Sick? What with?' Get hold of your syntax, Jennifer.

'He's got the 'flu like we had. He was up all night. He's asleep now, he doesn't know we're phoning you because we didn't think he'd let us. So we didn't tell him.'

'I'll come over right away.'

'I knew you would. Daniel didn't think you would, but I did.'

'Is everything else all right?'

'Oh yes. We've got swimming lessons this morning and then we have to get groceries and Daniel needs some scribblers for school.'

'Give me half an hour,' Jenny said. 'Can you manage until then?'

'We're getting breakfast. Daniel's making pancakes.'

'Tell him to be careful and I'll be there as soon as I can.'

Jenny had a quick shower, dressed in jeans and a shirt and drove into town. She pulled her car into the driveway behind Graham's, mentally thumbing her nose at Mrs Magnusson, and ran up the front steps. Neither door was locked. She walked in, heard voices from the kitchen and crossed the hall. At the kitchen door she paused, stunned.

Daniel had not confined his culinary ambitions to pancakes. Open boxes of cereal were scattered on the kitchen table. There was a strong smell of charred bacon in the air, and the tabby cat was disdainfully eyeing some small black scraps on the floor around the garbage can. The pancake mix, which was a dirty yellow colour, lay in blobs over the counter, the stove and much of Daniel's face.

Jason was under the table stuffing some brightly coloured cereal into his mouth. He was still in his pyjamas, the trousers of which were wet. Gillie was standing by the stove watching Daniel wield a metal spatula. His tongue clenched between his teeth, Daniel flipped a soggy-looking pancake up into the air, and as it miraculously fell back into the pan both children cheered.

They seemed in no imminent danger of setting themselves or the house on fire. Jenny turned around and went upstairs. Unmade beds, a dolls' tea party in progress on the floor in Gillie's room, a partially constructed skyscraper and an overturned box of bricks in Daniel's. Jason had been throwing blocks from his crib.

Amazing, Jenny decided, how much mess three children could make in such a short time!

The end door was ajar: Graham's door. She tiptoed towards it and peered inside.

His bedroom was large, with high, moulded ceilings and a bay window. The carpet and curtains were royal blue. Unlike the other bedrooms, it was very tidy, and unlike them, it was occupied. Graham was sprawled face down on the bed, only one arm and his head showing. He was deeply asleep. Jenny crept nearer, hearing the slow, heavy rhythm of his breathing, noticing how dark his hair was against the white pillow and how black his lashes in the pallor of his face. His complexion reminded her of Gillie's a few nights earlier.

Conquering the impulse to touch him, knowing he needed his sleep, she left the room as quietly as she had entered it and went downstairs. This time when she went to the kitchen door she announced her presence. 'Good morning!' she said. 'How are the pancakes?'

'Good,' said Daniel, stuffing a forkful into his mouth. 'There's lots left, Jenny—do you want some?'

Live dangerously, die young. 'Why not?' Jenny said. She made herself a cup of instant coffee and ate two pancakes; they exercised her jaws and her diplomatic skills, because Daniel was anxiously waiting for her opinion. 'You did a good job cooking them,' she said. 'Look how nice and brown they are.'

'Not half as brown as the bacon!' Gillie giggled.

'Shut up, Gillie,' Daniel ordered, dishing out the last two pancakes for himself and drowning them in syrup. 'You get to clean up because I did the cooking.'

'No way!' Gillie cried. 'Look at the mess you made.'

'We'll all help,' Jenny interjected. 'Tell me what has to be done today.'

While Daniel was emptying the rubbish and Gillie was rinsing the breakfast dishes, Jenny dived under the table to detach Jason from the cereal box. A pair of jeans-clad legs and two bare feet appeared in her field of vision. She blinked, and heard a man's voice say, 'Listen, kids, can one of you call Mrs Layton? Maybe she'll come over for part of the day. I can hardly stand up, let alone do anything useful . . .'

'Jenny's here,' Daniel said.

'*Jenny?* Where?'

Jenny poked her head from under the table and crawled out, her shirt gaping open to reveal her breasts. 'Here. Communing with your very damp son.' She got to her feet and stared at Graham in concern. 'I won't ask how you are.'

He was sagging against the doorframe, hair uncombed, chest bare; his face was haggard, his eyes sunk in their sockets like pieces of coal sunk into snow. 'I've felt better. What are you doing here?'

'Looking after the children for the day, because you're ill.'

His eyes moved to the two children at the sink. 'Which one of you phoned her?' he demanded, his voice unfriendly.

'Just be glad one of them had the sense to phone me,' Jenny put in. 'Because it's obvious you can't manage on your own.'

'We'll get Mrs Layton and then you can go home.'

She glared at him, forgetting their fascinated audience and the fact that he was ill. 'You will not! I have no plans for the day and I'd enjoy spending it with the children. Rather than being so ungrateful, you should be embracing me with fervour. Metaphorically, that is.'

'You'll have to settle for the metaphorical, I haven't got the strength for anything else . . . needing your help is getting to be a habit, Jenny Sprague.'

She said impishly, 'And a very nice one, too. By the look of you, you'd better go back to bed.'

He rubbed his forehead. 'I woke up and suddenly realised I didn't know where the children were or what they were up to. Could you get me a glass of water, Jenny?'

Daniel said, 'I'll make you a pancake, Dad.'

Graham suppressed a shudder. 'No, thanks, son—nothing against your pancakes, just against food in general.'

Jenny passed him a glass of water. There was a light film of sweat on his forehead; she had the feeling if the doorframe were not there, he would be flat on the floor. 'I'll help you upstairs,' she said. 'And don't argue.'

She looped an arm around his waist, braced herself for his weight and controlled various lecherous impulses at the feel of his bare skin under her fingertips. It was hot to the touch. 'You've got a fever,' she remarked.

He was concentrating on putting one foot after the other and did not bother answering her. He had to stop half-way up the stairs for a rest, his chest heaving. When they reached the top he said briefly, 'Bathroom.' Jenny left him at the door and crossed the hall to his room, where she had time to put on fresh pillowcases and make the bed before he appeared in the doorway. 'Thanks, Jenny,' he said. 'I do appreciate what you're doing.' Without self-consciousness he unzipped his jeans and stepped out of them, throwing them over the nearest chair.

Jenny tore her eyes away, busying herself adjusting the corner of the duvet. She was on the opposite side of the bed to Graham. He said, a hint of laughter in his voice, 'Come over here, it's a ten-mile hike round the end of the bed.'

She felt like a young girl on her first date rather than a twenty-five-year-old with an interesting history of

broken engagements. Watching her face, he added,
'You'll be quite safe.'

'*You* might not be,' she replied, walking slowly
around the end of the bed.

'Think of the children . . .'

She was standing only a few inches away from him.
He leaned forward, resting much of his weight on her.
'Sorry if I sounded ungrateful a few minutes ago,' he
mumbled. 'I'll rest better knowing the kids are in good
hands. I trust you with them, Jenny.'

'Thank you,' she whispered. His skin still felt hot; her
arms were beginning to ache.

'Hell, who am I kidding? It's not just a question of
trust. I'm more than half in love with you.'

His forehead had dropped to her shoulder. She stood
very still, wondering if she had dreamed those last few
words, knowing she had not, suffused with a happiness
as profound as it was—somewhere deep in her psyche—
frightening. She said with a touch of desperation,
'Graham, you're falling asleep on your feet.'

She felt him start. He pushed himself upright,
swaying a little, looking down at her as if he was not
quite sure who she was or what she was doing there. She
advised, more gently, 'You'd better get into bed.'

He sat down hard on the mattress and like a child
allowed her to pull the covers over him. Her feelings
could not have been described as maternal, however,
although she was aware of a deep tenderness as his head
fell back on the pillow and his eyes closed. Smoothing
his hair back from his forehead, she wondered if she
should call the doctor, and decided to wait until after
lunch. I'm more than half in love with you, he had said.
She was certain he would not have said those words if he
had not been light-headed with fever, and felt again that
uneasy mingling of joy and fear.

The children, she thought. You promised you'd look
after the children. Not stand around looking starstruck

because the father of those children might be falling in love with you. Move it!

Under Gillie's supervision the kitchen had been restored to order by the time Jenny went downstairs: counters wiped, dishwasher humming, all evidence of the pancakes removed. Jason's pyjama bottoms were in a sodden heap under the table. Of Jason there was no sign. Jenny declared approvingly, 'You did a great job, both of you—thanks. What time's the swimming lesson?'

'We got lots of time,' Daniel answered. 'We can take our bikes.'

'We'd better find our swimsuits,' Gillie said fussily. 'Come on, Daniel. Do you know where your goggles are?'

'Nope.'

'I'll help you look for them. And we've got to brush our teeth. Hurry up!' As Gillie herded Daniel out of the kitchen, Jenny smiled to herself. It was almost reassuring to see Gillie being self-important and—to put it bluntly—bossy; as her music teacher Jenny had only seen the better side of Gillie's character. Still smiling, she went in search of Graham's youngest child.

Jason, half-naked, was curled up on the chesterfield with the tabby cat, which wore an expression of long-suffering. When he saw Jenny, Jason said loudly, 'No, no, no,' and clutched the cat a little more tightly. The cat wriggled. 'Bad cat,' said Jason, digging his fists into its fur.

'Jason, you'd better let go——' Jenny began.

But she was too late. Using its back legs the cat levered itself off Jason's bare thigh and lunged for freedom, its ears laid back. Red claw marks appeared on Jason's skin. He grabbed for the cat's tail, fortunately missed it and said vengefully, 'Damn cat!' Then he looked up at Jenny pathetically, his blue eyes overflowing with tears, his lips wobbling. 'Bloody damn cat!' he cried.

She bit her lip to keep herself from laughing, wondering where he had overheard that particular phrase. 'You hurt the cat,' she said. 'So it hurt you. Let's go upstairs and find some clothes.'

Jason did not appreciate her lack of sympathy. 'Poor Jason,' he said, and the tears plopped on to his pyjama top. 'Bloody damn cat.' He put his head to one side, liking the sound of the words. 'Bloody damn cat.'

'Indeed,' Jenny said drily, deciding that no response was the best response, deciding also that Jason understood a great deal of what was going on around him. 'I'll put a bandage on your sore leg when we go upstairs.'

He gave her his sudden, entrancing smile and threw his arms around her neck. She picked him up, hoping he did not realise how her heart melted when he smiled like that. Like father, like son, she thought, settling him more comfortably on her hip. He had flecks of sugar on his chin and a dab of pancake mix on one ear. 'We'll have to wash you, too.'

'Bath,' Jason said in a tone that brooked no argument.

The bath involved a fleet of plastic boats, three rubber ducks, several sponges and a great deal of noise. Jason enjoyed himself thoroughly. Eventually, dried, powdered and clothed, he was sent from the bathroom while Jenny mopped it and herself up. As she wiped the mirror she smiled at her reflection, knowing that she, too, had enjoyed the bath.

In the hallway Gillie was still chivvying Daniel, who had not yet found his goggles. 'Come on, Daniel, you're so *slow*. Look, there they are, under those comics. Do *hurry*!'

Jenny started to make the beds. Daniel was not slow, she reflected; it was Gillie who was impatient.

Deliberate was a better way to describe Daniel. What a lot one could learn bringing up three children . . .

I'm more than half in love with you . . . she found herself clutching one corner of Gillie's blanket and longing with her heart to be part of this family with all its complex demands and equally complex rewards. So what did that mean? Was she, to use his own words, more than half in love with Graham? Or was he simply a means to an end? The man whose children could fill the emptiness in her soul?

She tucked in the blanket, plumped up the pillow and straightened the bedspread, and all the while her thoughts rambled on. Would she be as affected by Graham if he did not have children, a ready-made family that could become her own?

She genuinely did not know. Graham had children, they were an inseparable part of him. Yet at some deep level in her being he was her complement, the man who could answer her needs. She respected him. She liked him. She ached to make love with him. She stood still, holding Gillie's teddy bear in one hand. I love him, she thought, and felt clarity and joy envelop her. She sat down on the edge of the bed, still holding the teddy bear.

'Jenny, we're leaving now . . . Jenny—are you okay?'

She gaped at Daniel and Gillie, realising how silly she must look. 'I'm fine,' she stammered. 'Enjoy your lesson, won't you? Have you got everything you need?'

'Yep,' Daniel replied, brandishing his rolled-up towel. 'We'll be starving when we get home.'

She put the teddy bear with Gillie's dolls, where he sat like a sultan surrounded by his harem. 'I'll see what I can do. What's Jason up to, do you know?'

'Dunno,' Daniel answered. 'Dad says when he's quiet you better watch out.'

Hurriedly Jenny got up. 'I'll go and find him. See you later.'

Jason was in the hall. He had pulled the books out of

the lowest shelf of the bookcase and was peacefully leafing through a picture book, chattering away to himself; Jenny retreated quickly before she could disturb such a harmless activity.

By the time she had tidied the upstairs she had gathered at least one load of wash. She brought Jason downstairs, put the clothes in the washer, then did her best to draw up a grocery list. An indignant meow from the living-room sent her to the rescue of the tabby cat, again in Jason's clutches. She transferred the wash to the drier. She removed Jason from behind the chesterfield, where he had got wedged in pursuit of the cat. She swept the kitchen floor. She prevented Jason from eating a magazine. She started preparations for lunch, folded the wash and put it away. Then Daniel and Gillie came home.

What have I accomplished? Jenny wondered dazedly as she laid the kitchen table for lunch. Where did Mrs Layton find the time to polish floors and bake chocolate cakes?

After Jason had had a nap, Jenny took him grocery shopping. The cart was nearly full and the list completed when a red-haired woman in a flowered housedress came bustling around the corner. 'Why, Jason!' she gushed. 'And where is your father? Oh, hello, dear, you must be Dr Tyson's friend, Miss Sprague ... we haven't met, but I attended your delightful recital, such a pretty dress you wore that evening, I really don't blame Dr Tyson for being bowled over; if I've said to him once I've said to him a dozen times, "You need a good woman, Dr Tyson." But of course men are all the same, aren't they?' She thrust her heavily made-up face at Jason and cooed, 'Pretty baby. Pretty little baby.'

Jason leaned back as far as he could in the cart, scowled and said clearly, 'No, no, no.'

Said Jenny, who had recognised the red hair instantly even without the pruning shears, 'You must be Mrs Magnusson.'

'Elva Magnusson, that's right, dear, I live right across the street from Dr Tyson, such a fine man, isn't he?' She gave Jenny a coy, orange-lipsticked smile. 'I'm sure you agree. And where is he today?'

Jenny smiled back. 'He's home, I believe. Nice to have met you, Mrs Magnusson.' She mentally crossed her fingers to erase the lie.

'I'm sure I'll see you again,' said Mrs Magnusson archly.

I'm sure you will, thought Jenny. Through the curtain. She fled for the cash register.

The rest of the day proceeded smoothly; by nine o'clock that evening the children were all in bed and silence had descended on the house. Jenny cleared up the bathroom and the kitchen, then stood irresolutely at the foot of the stairs, wondering if she should leave now. It was nearly nine-thirty ... and she was tired.

Jason solved her dilemma by beginning to cry, a fussy little cry without much conviction. However, when nobody came to investigate, he put more energy into his efforts. Jenny did not want him waking the others. She went up to his room, changed him, then wrapped a blanket around him and sat in the armchair that stood in one corner of his room. He shoved his thumb in his mouth and let his head flop on her breast. Within minutes he was asleep.

Jenny settled herself more comfortably in the chair and let her thougnts drift. She was out on the marshes walking hand in hand with Graham when she heard a door open and the fall of footsteps. In a low voice she called, 'Graham? I'm in Jason's room.'

She had left the hall light on. When Graham came to the door his tall body was silhouetted against the light; he was wearing jeans and nothing else. 'Jenny?' he said uncertainly. 'It's late isn't it? You should have woken me.'

'Jason was fussing, that's why I'm still here.'

He came into the room, and as his eyes adjusted to the darkness he must have seen his son's dark head on Jenny's breast. He squatted beside the chair. 'What's the problem?'

'I think he just wanted some attention.'

'The others are in bed?'

She nodded. 'We had a good day.'

'So you've been here the whole day?' His voice sharpened. 'You should have called Mrs Layton, Jenny.'

'Shush, or you'll wake Jason,' she hissed. 'Anyway, we've been through all this before.'

'Put him to bed and we'll go downstairs. I need something to eat.'

'Not if we're going to fight,' she said stubbornly.

'So what are you going to do—sit there and hold him the whole night through? Here, give him to me, I'll put him to bed.'

As she relinquished her hold on Jason, Graham lifted him out of her arms. The moment had a peculiar poignancy for her, as if she was also relinquishing her tenuous hold on all of Graham's children. She stood up, stretched, and said with assumed calm, 'A cup of tea would hit the spot.'

Graham was covering Jason with a blanket. 'It sure would. I'll join you downstairs in a minute.' And he padded off in the direction of his bedroom.

Jenny put the kettle on the stove and stared aimlessly out of the window until Graham came into the kitchen. He had put on a shirt. He began opening cupboards and drawers, getting together cheese and crackers and a knife. 'You've had a long day,' he said non-committally.

She smiled. 'I'm wiped! Not used to looking after three children! But it was fun, I enjoyed it . . . I hope you don't find too many gaps in the grocery shopping.'

He cut himself a wedge of cheese. 'I'm feeling fine now, Jenny. You might as well leave, I'm sure you've got better things to do on a Saturday night than drink tea with me.'

She bit her lip. 'Are you being intentionally rude, or is it just your normal manner?'

'I'm not meaning to be rude at all, and I'm very appreciative of all you've done. But there's no need for you to stay—that's all I'm trying to say.'

Jenny poured boiling water over the tea bags and said frostily, 'Do you object if I have a cup of tea first?'

'Of course not. But what about Max?'

'What about him?'

'As I've already mentioned, it's Saturday night. Surely you have a date with him?'

'I was stood up.'

Graham sat down in the nearest chair and said irritably, 'My legs feel like rubber. What do you mean— stood up?'

Recklessly Jenny decided to burn her bridges. 'Max and I did have a date for tonight, you're quite correct. However, he heard that I'd spent the night with you last week. So he cancelled out.'

'Mrs. Magnusson!'

'Yes. As luck would have it I met her in the grocery store today . . . she recognised Jason, of course. And she knew my name.'

'God almighty! Didn't you tell Max nothing happened?'

'Of course I did. I also told him if I'd had my way something might well have happened.'

'You did, did you?' His eyes gleamed. 'I'm sure he didn't like that.'

'Not really. Max likes his women complaisant.'

'You do realise you've sidetracked me beautifully from the subject of Mrs Magnusson?'

'I rather thought so,' she answered with a touch of smugness, putting two mugs of tea on the table and sitting down across from him.

'Jenny, I loathe the thought of you being the subject of gossip which is not only malicious but also untrue.'

'I'm not crazy about it myself.'

'Which is a good reason why you should get in your car and go home now. It would seem I've already wrecked your relationship with Max.'

'You have, but not in the way you mean. The gossip was really nothing to do with it.'

There was a short silence. 'Jenny, don't fall in love with me.'

She looked him straight in the eye. 'Why not, Graham?'

'Because I'm not going to get married again. And I won't have an affair with you.'

'Yet you suggested you were more than half in love with me.'

'God—did I say that? I must have been delirious!'

'To have meant it or to have said it?'

He did not answer. 'Jenny, I've got nothing to give you.'

'You underrate yourself.'

'I'm being realistic. Associated with me are all the problems that go along with three children—none of whom are yours.'

Although Jenny's nerves tightened unconsciously, her face gave nothing away. 'But also all the joys that go with three children. Whether they're mine or not.'

'You can do one hell of a lot better than a thirty-four-year-old widower with three kids.'

'Maybe I don't want to do any better than that ' she said quietly

'Someone like Max, for instance.'

'Why do you think Max has no commitments and responsibilities? Because he can't handle them, that's why: I don't want Max, Graham. I wish you'd get that through your head.'

'You're not in love with him.'

He had made it a statement rather than a question, but she answered him anyway 'No, I'm not. I never have been. I never will be.'

As if he were repeating a lesson learned by rote, Graham added, 'And you don't want to go to bed with him.'

'Right. I had plenty of opportunity.'

'Max doesn't have any children.'

Up until now they had been fencing with each other, skirting around the main issue. Again Jenny felt that uncomfortable tightening of her nerves. 'Not as far as I know. So what?'

He pushed his chair back and stood up, going to lean against the counter. 'I've got three. A ready-made family for you.'

'What are you getting at, Graham?'

Graham's face was bleak. He said evenly, 'What's the attraction in the Tyson household? Me ... or Daniel, Gillie and Jason?'

She looked at him. 'That's hardly a fair question.'

'I think it's a very relevant question.'

What was she supposed to say ... I love you, Graham Tyson? Forthright she might be, but not that forthright. 'You're implying that I see you as a means to an end? How very convenient, here's a man with three children ... is that it?'

'You have to admit it fits. You can't have children. I've already got three. An ideal match.'

There were bruised shadows under his eyes. She hardened her heart. 'The word that would describe me is opportunist—isn't that what you're saying?'

'Don't be bitchy, Jenny! I'm trying to arrive at the truth.'

'Truth is one of those words like God. It has as many

meanings as there are people who use it.'

'So it *is* the children . . .'

'I don't want to go to bed with the children!' she flared.

For a moment his frown relaxed. 'The sexual attraction between us we can take as given. No arguments there. No, it's more than that, Jenny.'

'I don't *know*!' she cried, hounded. 'I loved holding Jason this evening and watching him fall asleep in my arms. I have a very special affinity for Gillie. I like all your children and being with them today filled a—an emptiness in my soul. I can't deny that.'

'Funny . . . I never thought I'd find a woman who'd be willing to take on all my children. I now find one who'd probably be more than willing and I'm complaining.'

'The children exist,' she whispered. 'How can I separate them from you?' This was true, as far as it went. Tell me how you feel about me, she pleaded inwardly. But don't expect me to expose all my feelings unless you're prepared to do the same.

He was not—she could tell. Confusion and exhaustion greyed his features and flattened his voice as he said, 'Jenny, the timing's all wrong. I sense in you a lot of bitterness still, towards Marc and Samuel, and towards your inability to have children. God knows, there's been bitterness in me as far as Mona's concerned, bitterness and guilt and the sensation of having failed her, of never having been enough for her . . . Apart from all that, I'm nearly ten years older than you. And you're new to Brockton, you've scarcely got your sea legs yet.'

He stopped rather abruptly. She said the only thing that came into her head. 'I think you should sit down.'

'I think you should go home, Jenny.'

She felt ice-cold and very frightened. 'And stay out of your life—is that the message?'

'For a while I believe it would be wise for you to do just that.'

Clutching at straws, she blurted, 'But what about Gillie's piano lessons?'

'I'll drop her off and you can bring her home. You and I don't have to see each other.'

'Do you dislike me that much?'

'If I disliked you, life would be simple . . . go home, Jenny. And thank you for everything you've done today.'

At some point in the conversation he had walked back to the table. Now he gave her a pat on the shoulder which she was sure he intended to be brotherly. But by mistake his palm fell partly on the open neck of her shirt, his thumb brushing her smooth, warm flesh. His face constricted. With a groan he pulled her to her feet, tipped her face and found her lips in a kiss of such desperation that Jenny felt the tears flood her eyes; he was kissing her as if he were a dying man bidding his last farewell, as if he would never see her again or hold her in his arms or taste the sweetness of her mouth.

He pushed her away, grabbing the nearest chair for support. 'Go home, Jenny—please,' he said hoarsely.

She was trembling, a battle raging within her. Tell him you love him and see what he says, urged one little voice.

Run, Jenny . . . or are you courting rejection number three? countered the other.

Afterwards, she was convinced she would have run, because there was too much past history to have done otherwise. But at the time Jason saved her from a decision by emitting a long, mournful cry that carried all the way down the stairs. 'I'll go,' Graham said quickly. 'Because we've said it all, haven't we, Jenny?'

She allowed her misery and confusion to show in her face. 'You seem to think we have, Graham. I'm not so sure.'

'We have.' Another cry from upstairs, louder and more imperative. 'Take care of yourself,' he said flatly, and left the room.

Moving like an old woman, Jenny went in search of her handbag and her car keys. She let herself out of the front door and clumped down the steps, which wavered through the tears in her eyes. She got in her car, blew her nose and backed out of the driveway. As she drove away, the net curtains in the Victorian house that belonged to Mrs Magnusson twitched back into place.

CHAPTER NINE

DURING the next few days Jenny went over that conversation between her and Graham line by line, wresting from each sentence a variety of meanings depending on her mood. Since her mood was predominantly miserable, the prognosis was not optimistic.

Graham wanted to take her to bed, she never doubted that. But he did not want to marry her. His previous marriage had been unhappy, certainly. But had he loved her he would have wanted to marry her despite his problems with Mona, because theirs would be, to use his own words, an ideal match. Therefore he did not love her, a conclusion which brought her no joy.

Moreover, he suspected her of using him. She wrestled with this as well, searching her own motives and emotions, trying very hard to be absolutely honest, and the conclusion she came to was that because Graham had children, it was an ideal match for her—but only because she loved him for himself. If Max had three children, a thought that boggled her mind, she would not have married him. She wanted Graham, with or without children. With was a bonus. But it did not seem as though she was going to have him.

Gillie's first piano lesson was not a good experience. Gillie was to arrive by seven o'clock. By six-thirty Jenny had eaten supper, cleaned the kitchen and found the music she wanted them to work on. She had put on her favourite jumpsuit and rather a lot of perfume, just in case Graham came in with Gillie; perched on the arm of one of the chairs, she watched the road.

At five to seven the BMW turned into the driveway.

Gillie got out and closed the door. The car reversed and drove away.

Graham had not waved or even looked in Jenny's direction. Within her, anger warred with pain, and professionalism won: she had a job to do, a music lesson to conduct for a highly gifted pupil. She would bawl her eyes out after Gillie was gone.

But Gillie's departure, of course, entailed Jenny driving her home. Lights shone from the windows of the grey and white house; Jenny had to fight with herself not to follow Gillie up the steps. 'See you next week,' she said brightly.

Gillie gave a little skip of pure joy. 'I loved our lesson. Thank you, Jenny.'

Some of the hurt was assuaged for Jenny—but only some of it, The rest she carried home with her, where, true to her word, she indulged in a good cry.

The pattern was the same the following week. The day after Gillie's second lesson Max took Jenny to the local inn for lunch, the meeting he had suggested two weeks earlier. They ordered fish chowder and home-made rolls, the speciality of the house, then Max said with a lift of his brow, 'So, Jenny, how are you?'

'Do you want me to say fine, thank you, or do you want the truth?'

He puffed up his chest. 'I'm man enough to take the truth.' But there was concern behind his smile, as well as—thought Jenny—a measure of self-interest.

'Miserable,' she said succinctly.

'Your friend Graham is not coping with the twentieth century as cleverly as he does the eighteenth?'

'Stop trying to be cute,' she said crossly. 'We're not seeing each other at all.'

'You look as though it was a year-long love affair, not a matter of three—it was three, wasn't it?—dates.'

'I feel as though it was for ever.'

He began to butter a roll. 'Try one of these. Starving

yourself won't help.'

'How do you know I haven't been eating well?'

'I have eyes, Jenny. You've lost about five pounds since I saw you last.' Again he quirked his brow. 'Right?'

'Right.' Glumly she helped herself to a pat of butter. 'I don't feel like eating. I don't feel like doing anything very much.'

'So what's the problem?'

'He has three kids, hang-ups about his wife and my career, and thinks he's too old for me. Will that do for a start?'

'I have no kids, no previous wife or hang-ups, and am in the prime of my life.' He grinned at her. 'Won't I do instead? Because I, sugarplum, am willing!'

She patted his hand. 'You're good for my ego, Max— thanks. But no, thanks.'

'Figured I should try, at least.' Briskly he buttered another portion of bread. 'So what are we going to do about this? We can't have you languishing away to a mere shadow of your former self.'

Max had anticipated her refusal; Jenny gave a tiny sigh of relief. 'There's nothing can be done,' she said. 'That's one of the reasons I feel so rotten—because I'm helpless. Powerless. Graham has made up his mind and that's that.'

'Minds can be changed, sugarplum. Even when they belong to a man as proud as Graham Tyson.'

'Proud?'

'Sure. Hell, if I had half a dozen squalling brats, do you think I'd be hanging around you? Not likely!'

'Three is not half a dozen. And I love . . .' Jenny faltered to a stop. 'I love his children,' she finished more firmly. 'Who are *not* squalling brats!'

Max warded off an imaginary blow. 'Okay, okay. I apologise.' The waitress, who was approaching with their chowder, understandably looked a little startled;

he gave her his most charming smile. When she was out of earshot he went on, 'Why don't you and I start dating again—very publicly? It'll make Graham so jealous he'll forget all his scruples and ask you to marry him.' He passed her the salt and pepper. 'That's what you want, isn't it?'

'Yes. But it wouldn't work, Max. He'd think you were a much better deal.'

'Why don't we start dating again anyway?'

She looked at him, her spoon halfway to her mouth. 'When you know I'm—I'm obsessed with somebody else? Come off it, Max,'

'Don't be so quick off the mark, Jenny, my love.' He smiled at her with engaging frankness. 'I haven't met anyone else who interests me nearly as much as you do. They all seem a bit insipid after you. Or maybe—like you—I only want what I can't have.'

Troubled, Jenny gazed down at her chowder, as if the chunks of potato and fish would give her an answer to her dilemma. 'But, Max——'

'Jenny, I'm willing to settle for whatever you're able to give. No pressure, no strings, no games. And I don't want you feeling guilty because you can't give me as much as you think I want—I can look after myself.'

'I . . . don't know. I don't understand how in so short a time Graham has become so deeply and irrevocably a part of me. There's no sense to it . . . and certainly no reward,' she finished with a tinge of bitterness.

'So, forget it for a while! Concentrate on my undoubted charms instead.'

'You can always make me laugh, Max, I give you that.'

'Maxwell the clown, that's me.'

He was not meeting her eyes. In swift compunction she said, 'Max, I meant that as a compliment, I didn't mean to hurt you.'

'Let's get something straight, Jenny. I'm not in love

with you. Intrigued by you and lusting after you, yes—but not in love.'

She gave him her first real smile. 'Men are very complicated creatures.'

'Almost as complicated as women.'

'*Amadeus* is coming here next week. We could go and see it.'

'It's a date.'

She took a mouthful of the chowder, which was delicious, and hoped she was doing the right thing. But if Graham didn't want her, why should she sit around in widow's weeds?

In a town the size of Brockton and a university as small as St Martin's, it was inevitable that Jenny and Graham meet. This meeting did not occur, however, for nearly three weeks, and the place, the car park of the supermarket, was scarcely fortuitous. Graham was getting out of his car just as Jenny was walking over to hers with an armload of groceries. He saw her, hesitated, then said prosaically, 'Give me the groceries, Jenny, while you unlock the trunk.'

She seemed to be frozen to the spot. Her eyes devoured him, seeing every detail of the dark, springing hair, the deep blue eyes, the tall, rangy body. She swallowed. 'Hello, Graham.'

In a low voice intended for her ears alone he said, 'Have you ever made love in the car park of a grocery store?'

'I can't say I have.'

'Then stop looking at me like that. Or you will be!'

A box with very sharp corners was digging into her stomach. 'I dare you,' she said.

His smile was wry. 'You called my bluff. You've lost weight, Jenny.'

'Unrequited love,' she murmured.

He took the two brown bags from her arms. 'Love,

Jenny?' he said quizzically.

'That's the word I used. You don't look so great yourself—what's your excuse?'

He frowned. 'Why don't you unlock the trunk?'

'Why don't you answer the question?'

'Because I have nothing new to add to what I've already said. Besides, you're dating Max again, aren't you?'

She felt anger and pain flick along her nerves. 'Again?' she said coldly. 'We never really stopped.'

He glared at her. 'If you don't unlock the truck I'll put the groceries on the ground and walk away.'

'You're behaving very childishly,' she chided.

'It's the effect you have on me.'

'Do you know the effect you have on me? I feel as though I've been jilted without having been engaged. As though you've turned me down without even bothering to get to know me.'

'Oh, I've always known you.' said Graham gravely.

She could not doubt his sincerity. With a helpless gesture of bewilderment she fumbled for her keys and unlocked the trunk. After Graham had put the bags of groceries in, she slammed the lid shut. 'Thank you,' she said. 'Don't let me hold you up.'

'You haven't asked how the children are.'

'I don't need to. Gillie keeps me in touch.'

'You didn't get the 'flu?'

'No.'

As he stared down at her, passers by glanced at them curiously. They made a striking couple, he so tall and dark, she curved and ripely blonde—but more than that, the tension between them was palpable, had they been screaming at each other they could not have been more openly in conflict. As if he could not help himself, Graham said, 'I'm about as popular as a skunk with the children right now.'

Jenny should have bade him a cool and dignified

farewell, got in her car and driven away. Instead she said, 'Oh . . . why?'

'Because you never come to the house.'

'I hope you told them it's because I haven't been invited.'

'I did. Talk about disapproval!'

'If they all hated me you'd be using *that* as the reason you and I can't see each other. That they all like me seems to be just as much of an excuse! I'll never understand you, Graham Tyson!'

'It's not that they like you—it's that you love them. You notice I used the word love.'

The breeze stirred her hair. 'It's the correct word,' she said, raising her chin.

'I've had a lot of time to think since I last saw you, Jenny. The reason we're an ideal match is that I make you an instant mother. Three children, all yours. That's it, isn't it?'

'Do you want me to say I'm not the slightest bit interested in being a mother? You know and I know that's not true.'

His face hardened. 'Let me tell you something about Mona, and then maybe you'll understand why I'm not punching Max in the jaw, throwing you over my shoulder and carrying you off to the nearest Justice of the Peace.'

If there had not been such an undertone of menace in his voice she might have been amused; as it was, she waited in silence, unconsciously bracing herself for whatever was to come.

'I loved Mona when I married her. I thought she loved me. Maybe she did . . . I don't know. She wanted to have a family and that was fine with me, I've always liked children. Just three months after we were married she got pregnant with Gillie. Perhaps I had a few thoughts that it would have been better to wait for a while, to have got to know each other better before

adding the complication of a baby . . . but I was happy,
too. I had my Ph.D. and my first teaching post. I was in
love with my wife, and we were expecting our first
child. All was well with the world.'

His eyes were faraway, focused on another time and
another place. 'And then Gillie was born, and Mona
began to change. I thought it was natural enough at first
that she be wrapped up in the baby; she'd had a hard
time with the pregnancy and a difficult birth, and she
deserved to enjoy our new daughter. But I soon began to
realise that she was obsessed with the child to the
exclusion of all else—including me. For months
afterwards she didn't want to make love. It hurt, she
said. The truth was, the doctor had told her she mustn't
get pregnant again, and not until Jason was conceived
did she ever show any real interest in me as far as sex
was concerned. Making love was for making babies,
that was her rationale . . . she wouldn't get babysitters
because Gillie might cry, and she wouldn't go on
holidays because Gillie's routine would be upset, on and
on it went, until I was nearly frantic! Then my cousin
and his wife were killed and we adopted Daniel. I
thought it would break her total absorption in Gillie,
and so it did. She now had two to be absorbed in, not
one. And never again did I have the feeling that I was
necessary to Mona or that she loved me for myself. Oh, I
was useful. I paid the bills, I kept a roof over her head, I
paid for the children's clothes and food and toys. But
beyond that she didn't seem to *see* me, or to realise that I
might have needs exclusive of those of the children.
And when I tried to object to the way our marriage had
evolved, she was always so damned reasonable that I
ended up feeling like a monster for daring to criticise
the sacred cult of motherhood. Do you understand at all,
Jenny—or do you think I was totally selfish?'

Jenny was beginning to see the drift of the conversation. She became aware of a strong dislike for Mona,

who had not loved Graham enough, and could not chide herself for disliking a dead woman. 'Of course I understand.'

'I loved the children!' he burst out. 'But we needed a life of our own, and we never had that ... well, you know the rest. Jason was born and Mona died. I had tried to keep on loving her, she was my wife. But somewhere along the way the love had died as well.' He dragged his eyes back to Jenny's face. 'You're intelligent enough to realise where all this is leading. I can see the attraction my children would have for you—and it terrifies me. I will not play second fiddle to my children again, Jenny.'

'That's a neat game, Graham. If you meet someone who does like your children, you won't marry her because you might come second. If you meet someone who doesn't, she wouldn't be suitable anyway. A no-win situation—for the woman!'

'Okay, so I'm afraid of getting married again,' he snarled. 'In the position I'm in I have to play it safe. Because the feelings of four people are involved here— not just mine.'

'Five, I would have said. What about the unfortunate woman?'

He ignored her comment. 'If the kids got really attached to you—because we're talking about you, aren't we, not some mythical woman—and then you and I called it off, they'd be devastated.'

'You can't call off something that never got started,' Jenny said furiously.

Graham stepped closer and said in a low, ferocious voice, 'Do you think I don't know that? I'd like to take you home right now and spend a week in bed with you and then see if we can still stand the sight of each other. That's what I'd like to do. But I can't, Jenny—because I'm not free. The children watch me like a hawk. They like you. They'd love it if you moved in. But what if it didn't work out? What then? How would I tell them? How would I make them understand?' He gave her a shake. 'They'd be hurt! And—except for Jason, who never knew his mother—they've been hurt before. I can't do it, Jenny. I *won't* do it!'

'You're making your own prison! You're hiding behind the children——' She broke off, his fists clenched at her sides. A woman was unlocking the hatchback in the next car. From somewhere Jenny summoned a more normal voice. 'Oh, excuse me, are we in your way?'

Graham pointedly looked at his watch. 'I've got to go, Jenny.'

She gave him a brittle smile, hating him and loving him in equal measure, wanting to stamp on his toes yet also to throw her arms around him and kiss him. 'So must I. I'd better not keep Max waiting, had I?' She was not seeing Max for another three hours, but Graham was not to know that.

'No, I don't think you should keep Max waiting.' His voice was even, his words fraught with more significance than she wished to hear.

The words burst out through no volition of her own. 'Graham, leave out everyone else—Max, Mona, the children and Mrs Magnusson—what do *you* want in all this?'

'You, of course,' he said simply.

The woman had backed out of the parking space next to Jenny's and another car had driven in, a car crammed with teenagers and reverberating with rock music. A young man with a lock of turquoise hair and a single gold earring leaned out of the window and called out, 'Hiya, Beautiful,' to Jenny. She was not flattered.

'I'm as likely to marry that young man as I am to marry Max,' she said. 'But I'm obviously even less likely to marry you. Goodbye, Graham.'

He was still standing beside the neighbouring car as

she reversed and drove on to the street, her emotions a
delicate balance between fury, frustration and tears.

CHAPTER TEN

Two weeks passed. Gillie had her piano lessons, Jenny lectured and read and marked papers, and thought about Graham incessantly. Max, fortunately, was being a model escort, making no demands on her but making her laugh, for both of which she was grateful, although she was certainly clever enough to realise he was not being strictly altruistic. Max had designs on her, but Max was prepared to wait.

Then, on a Friday afternoon at about four-thirty, Jenny had a visitor. She was in her office in the Music building marking a batch of essays from her piano literature course, not an altogether pleasurable task. There were two brilliant papers, several entirely acceptable ones, and a few that made her fear for the future of English grammar and the status of music. She was fighting her way through a maze of misplaced clauses supposedly describing ornamentation in the baroque period when a tap came at the door. She looked up, red pen in hand, hoping for the sake of the supplicant that he or she was not a student. 'Come in.'

The woman who entered was a stranger to her, yet somehow familiar—tall, with upswept dark hair and glorious blue eyes very adeptly made up. The woman said in a friendly, brisk voice, 'Are you Jennifer Sprague?' Jenny nodded. 'I'm Helen Walters. Graham Tyson's sister.'

Jenny put down the pen and forgot about ornamentation. 'You're very like him,' she said slowly. 'Please sit down, Mrs Walters.'

'Call me Helen, please,' was the reply. 'In view of why I've come to see you, I think we should waive formality!' She indicated the heap of essays. 'I can see I'm

162

interrupting, but I'm not going to apologise. Unless I'm totally mistaken, you'll consider the interruption justified.'

Jenny said sharply, 'They're all right, are they—Graham and the children?'

'Apart from the fact that Graham looks like death warmed over, yes. I'm staying for the weekend, so I've sent him packing, he needed a break from family and housework.' She gave Jenny a disarming smile. 'As I'm sure you know, he's far too conscientious; I had quite an argument on my hands before he'd go away.'

The same strength of jaw-line was evident in Helen as in Graham; Jenny would have liked to have been a fly on the wall during that argument. 'So why are you here?' she asked pleasantly, quite sure that Helen was one for the direct approach.

'Graham's in love with you—you know that?'

By a mammoth effort Jenny did not as much as blink. 'Give me one good reason why I should answer that question,' she said warmly.

'Because unless I'm very much mistaken, the two of you are made for each other. Graham needs you. The children need you. And you need them.'

'You've got a real nerve!' Jenny exclaimed, not sure whether she liked Graham's sister or not. 'Three minutes ago you hadn't even met me!'

Helen crossed long, elegant legs. 'Let me put you in the picture. I'm four years younger than Graham and I have the good fortune to be married to a very successful stockbroker whom I happen to love. He's the head of his firm, an expert in management, and he says I'm a born dictator. You can decide whether or not you agree with him. We live in Toronto, by the way. I haven't seen Graham for over a year, and I was horrified by the way he looked when I arrived last night. My brother can be the most taciturn of men, as you probably know, but by the time we'd worked our way through the bottle of Chivas Regal I'd brought with me, I'd wormed the whole story out of him—the beautiful young professor who was giving Gillie lessons in piano, and him, if you'll pardon the banality, lessons in love.' Helen leaned forward, suddenly very serious. 'Jenny, Mona was one of the most persuasive arguments against marriage and motherhood that I know of. I know she was my sister-in-law and I tried very hard to like her, but I hated what she did to Graham. She shut him out. She killed his spontaneity and his sense of fun—his youth, if you like. All in the most high-minded and sanctimonious way. She tried her best to keep him from the children, but there she didn't succeed—he's always been devoted to them and wouldn't allow her to push him to the sidelines . . . so if he's afraid of risking intimacy again, there's a good reason.'

Helen paused, apparently expecting Jenny to comment. But she merely gave a self-possessed nod. Folding her hands in her lap, Helen went on confidently, 'I gather Graham's already told you about our somewhat disordered childhood. Being the elder, he bore the brunt of it. He told me last night that although, like our father, you're a pianist, you've handled your career very differently. Graham is now—thanks to you—able to accept that Gillie may well be headed for a career as a professional pianist.'

'Graham must have drunk a fair bit last night,' Jenny commented coolly.

'A fair bit. I drank my share, too,' Helen added with a touch of complacency. 'Anyway, he's obviously resolved any conflicts he had about your job, so that gets rid of that objection.'

'Objection to what, Helen?'

'Your marriage!' Helen replied, surprised.

'If Graham suggested to you that he's asked me to marry him, then he really was drunk. The opposite is nearer the truth—he's spent a great deal of time convincing me why it's impossible for us to marry. Without ever taking the risk of asking me.'

'He's afraid you love the children more than him.'

The Chivas Regal must have been powerful stuff. 'That's true—he is. But he's never asked me if I love him.'

'You do. I can tell.'

'You don't happen to be a lawyer, do you? Or a psychiatrist? You seem to be leading me on beautifully. Yes, I do. But how do I prove it? How can I prove I'd love Graham if he didn't have as much as one child? Answer me that, Helen.' Jenny's voice was trembling. She picked up the red pen and doodled fiercely on her notepad.

'Certainly. I have a plan.'

Somehow Jenny was not surprised. 'What *do* you do for a living, Helen?'

'I run an employment agency. A very successful one.'

Jenny's curiosity got the better of her. 'So what's the plan?'

'One of the other history professors has a cabin in the woods about sixty miles from here. Glorious country-side, hills, streams, trees, deer, trout—a superfluity of nature in its most untamed state.'

'But you prefer Toronto.'

'Nature always seems to involve getting your feet wet and being bitten by mosquitoes.' Fastidiously Helen straightened the collar of her silk blouse with a hand on which a sapphire glowed. 'But Graham loves it up there—says it gets him away from it all. He's there now. He's not due back until Sunday afternoon. I suggest you drive up there tonight, preferably after dark—which will impress him no end because it really is the backwoods—and tell him you came to see him, not the children, and that you can't drive back tonight so you'll have to stay over.' Thoughtfully Helen considered the sapphire. 'Our mother came from good Puritan stock, morals as straight as a gun barrel and just about as deadly. So Graham places a great deal of importance on such matters as reputation.'

'But if it's in the backwoods, nobody will know I'm there.'

'He will.'

'Helen, this is all very clever, but the differences between Graham and me are a little too deep to be solved by an escapade in the woods.'

Helen gave her a bland look. 'You mean you're scared to try?'

'Subtle,' said Jenny sarcastically.

'Do you want him or don't you?'

Jenny's eyes fell first. 'Yes, I do.'

'If you drive up to the cabin it can't do any harm. And it might even do some good. But that's only the first phase of the plan.'

'What's the second?' Jenny asked in a resigned tone of voice.

Helen smirked. 'Oh, the second phase is up to you . . . Graham told me how charmingly you blush, I see he didn't exaggerate. The third phase is this: the next morning I'll drive up to the cabin with the children. The children are not pleased with their father. This morning before they left for school they drew up a list of all the reasons why he should marry you. They think it's a wonderful scheme to drive up to Trout Brook—that's where the cabin is—and present this list to both of you.' Helen tipped her head to one side. 'Phase four should be a party, don't you think?'

Jenny stared down at the swirling red lines on the notepad. 'Helen, seriously, do you think Graham loves me? We haven't seen that much of each other, you know. And when we do get together, all we seem to do is fight.'

'At two o'clock this morning—or it might have been two-thirty—he was certainly acting like a man quite hopelessly in love.'

'*In vino veritas?*'

'*In* Chivas Regal *veritas!*'

Jenny took a deep breath. 'In the course of all this

alcoholic imbibing, he must have told you that I can
never have children?' Helen nodded. 'He thinks I'm
using him, Helen. That rather than loving *him*, I only
want his family.'

'Perfectly understandable, after Mona. And after all,
you never told him you loved him—did you?'

'No! There are limits to honesty.'

'So instead—I'm only guessing here—you've spent a
month of perfect misery, and so has he. Time something
was done.' Suddenly Helen smiled, a smile so like
Graham's that Jenny's heart skipped a beat. 'I love my
brother, Jenny. He went to bat for me on more than one
occasion against my parents. I'd do anything in the
world to make him happy.'

Jenny let out her breath in a long sigh and decided she
liked Helen Walters very much. 'You'd better tell me
how to get to this place, Trout Brook.'

'I've drawn you a map.' Helen frowned a little. 'It's
supposed to rain fairly heavily later on, but only the last
eight miles or so is on dirt roads, the rain shouldn't be a
problem.' She reached into her very beautiful leather
handbag and took out a piece of paper.

Dubiously Jenny looked at the spidery lines meander-
ing over the page, lines adorned with an assortment of
little arrows, numbers and hieroglyphs. 'It looks very
complicated.'

'Not really. You start out in Moncton and you turn
right . . .'

Jenny listened, made Helen repeat herself, and said
doubtfully, 'I think I've got it.'

'I'm sure you have. You can always ask directions if
you get lost.' Helen pushed the paper across the desk to
Jenny. 'So you'll do it?'

Something about the scheme appealed to the roman-
tic streak in Jenny: to arrive at her lover's log cabin in
the darkness of an autumn storm, to be swept into his
arms . . . it was a pity she couldn't wear a long dress.
Green velvet, she thought dreamily, with a décolletage

and lots of white lace . . .

'I'll arrive with the children about eleven in the morning . . . Jenny, are you listening?'

'Oh—yes, I'm listening.'

'Just so we won't catch you in bed,' Helen added suavely.

'If Graham realises the whole thing is a set-up, you might catch me in the woodshed!' Jenny countered, managing not to blush this time. 'Eleven o'clock. Okay.'

'Good. What time will you leave this evening?'

She considered. 'No later than eight. I should allow an hour and a half to get there.'

Helen stood up. 'I'll let you get on with your work. I've enjoyed meeting you, Jenny, and I'll see you again tomorrow. Good luck.' Solemnly they shook hands across the desk, then Helen left the office, closing the door behind her with a decisive snap.

Jenny looked at the map and the swirling red doodles. She looked at the last page she had marked on the essay, with its dangling participles, its double negatives and incorrect pronouns. She put the red pen in her drawer and stood up. If she was going to Trout Brook she had more important things to consider than baroque ornamentation and faulty sentences. To start with, as a green velvet dress was out of the question, she had to decide what to wear.

She eventually settled on a royal blue jumpsuit with a wide black sash and black slingback shoes: a concession to the backwoods without surrendering a certain sophistication. The open neckline could be adjusted to levels ranging from prudish to wanton; the sash emphasised the satisfactory smallness of Jenny's waist; the lacy black underwear she wore underneath was not chosen for warmth. She took a raincoat, a pair of rubber boots and a toothbrush. She did not take a nightdress.

At seven-thirty she left the house. Although it was not raining, the wind was blowing in fitful gusts so that the low-hanging clouds scudded across the sky. It was

already dark. She checked that she had the map and
turned on to the Trans-Canada Highway.

Such was the power of Helen's personality that Jenny
had given very little thought to the success or failure of
her mission. Now, as her car sped along the highway
and the first raindrops spattered on the windscreen, she
began to worry. Gall, effrontery, nerve ... all those
words would apply to Helen's scheme. Not to mention
lunacy! Graham, who had gone to the cabin in the
woods for peace and quiet, would have every right to
send her straight back to Brockton. Or, she thought
ruefully, to banish her to the woodshed. After all, she
only had Helen's word that he loved her, and at the time
of Graham's confession Helen had been matching her
brother drink for drink. Perhaps Helen had misunder-
stood, or heard what she had wanted to hear, or had
falsified her account for reasons of her own. As Jenny
drove through the darkness she realised that although
she liked Helen, she did not totally trust her.

She negotiated the rain-wet streets of Moncton,
crossed the bridge and turned right. So far, so good. The
route numbers on the white signs at the side of the road
matched the numbers on the map, and although it was
raining harder, the road was hard-surfaced and in good
shape. Her car purred along smoothly. On the radio
Placido Domingo and John Denver sang of love, and to
soothe her nerves Jenny sang along with them.

At the next crossroads she turned right, then left at
the T-junction and right at the fork in the road by the
church. A terrific map, she thought exultantly, knowing
she would be arriving on Graham's doorstep within the
half-hour. Clever Helen. Brave Jenny. Wonderful
Graham . . .

The road divided into two. Jenny slammed on the
brakes and consulted the map. According to the map
the road should not have divided into two; some of her
euphoria evaporated. She peered through the windscreen. Not a house or a building in sight, no signposts,

and the telephone poles went both ways.

She frowned at the map. Generally speaking she had been keeping to the right; maybe she should go right again. She flicked on her signal light, even though there was no one behind her, and took the right-hand road. When she had gone a couple of miles, still without seeing a house, the tarmac ended. But the dirt surface was wide and well graded, so Jenny drove on. A mile further on she came to a crossroads. A drunken signpost bore the names of three places, none of which was mentioned on the map. Jenny debated turning around, then down the left-hand fork saw the distant glimmer of lights. Lights meant people, and people meant information. She turned left. The lights came from a little village boasting a small brick post office with a wet flag tangled around the flagpole, a gas station, closed, and a general store, open. Jenny pulled up in front of the store, put her raincoat around her shoulders and ran for the door.

The proprietor was a very old man, stooped and wrinkled, his clothing as fusty as the air in the store. He was also very deaf. Jenny explained her destination as best she could, trying to speak slowly, loudly and distinctly.

'Trout Brook?' he echoed, holding the map close to his nose with a hand that shook. 'Trout Brook's over the mountain.' Vaguely he gestured at the shelves of canned goods behind him. 'That a'way.'

'How far?' Jenny yelled.

'I dunno. Three, four miles maybe. But the road ain't so good.'

'If I go back to the crossroads which way do I go?'

'You can't get to Trout Brook from there.' He peered at her suspiciously. 'Not much goin' on in Trout Brook this time o'night.'

With a sinking heart Jenny realised Helen had neglected to mention the name of the professor who owned the cabin. 'I'm visiting a friend,' she shouted, hoping that her neckline covered her decently; the old man's eyes had a tendency to wander. 'I'll go straight up the hill, then.'

'They don't call it Breakheart Hill for nothin'.' He pulled an old-fashioned watch from his pocket. 'Time to close up. You gonna buy anythin'?'

She bought two of the freshest looking chocolate bars and a can of pop, the top of which had a thin film of dust on it. As she went down the steps the old man slammed the door shut behind her and turned out the light. She scurried round the car and collapsed in her seat. To give herself courage she ate one of the chocolate bars. It was stale. Then she started the motor, turned on the wipers and headed up Breakheart Hill.

For the first half mile or so she thought the old man had been exaggerating, because the road was in passable condition and there were houses scattered on either side of it. But then, abruptly, it narrowed, trees closing in on either side. Water rolled in the ditches, where it belonged, but it had also gouged runnels in the road and eaten away the mud shoulders. Jenny clutched the steering wheel and kept to the middle of the track, hearing rocks rattle against the underside of her car and feeling the wheels grab for a purchase in the gravel. For the first time since she had left Brockton, Graham was not uppermost in her mind.

The incline grew steeper and the road narrower. In the beam of her headlights she saw spruce boughs tossing in the wind and moss-covered boulders as big as her piano. Logging roads vanished into the blackness. Perhaps the old man had been playing a cruel joke on her, and at the top of the mountain this road too would turn into a sea of mud indented with bulldozer tracks and edged with piles of pulpwood.

But she was doing him an injustice. The road levelled out at the top of the mountain and as the wind buffeted the car and the rain lashed the windshield, the slope began to head downwards. A downward slope presupposed a valley, and a valley a brook. A brook with trout

in it, Jenny thought optimistically, and a log cabin on
the side of a hill where a dark-haired man would
welcome her with open arms. Please God, she thought
frantically, as the car juddered down a grade corrugated
like cardboard and she fought to control the wheel, let
him be pleased to see me.

The road came to an abrupt end after a hairpin turn,
and once again Jenny was faced with the choice of a
right or a left-hand turn. A makeshift tar-paper shack
with two old cars and a truck parked outside faced her
on the opposite side of the road, yellow light shining
from the front windows. The strain of Breakheart Hill
had told on Jenny. She was tired and anxious to get to
her destination, in no mood to drive around the back
roads searching for Graham's cabin. Resolutely she
pulled behind one of the cars, buttoned up her raincoat
and ran up the plank walk to the front door. She could
hear the rumble of masculine voices. Raising her fist,
she banged on the door.

The voices were cut off in mid-sentence; all Jenny
could hear was the rain dripping from the eaves and the
sough of the wind in the trees. She almost turned and
hurried back to the car, for there was a waiting quality
to the silence that unnerved her. However, she firmed
her lips and knocked on the door again.

It swung open so quickly that the man must have
been standing on the other side of it all the time. He had
a black beard and a belly that strained at the buttons of
his checked wool shirt. When he saw her, an expression
that could have been relief briefly lifted his dour
features. 'Yeah?' he said.

'I'm looking for Trout Brook. Please can you tell me
which way I should go?'

At the sound of her clear, high-pitched voice three
other men crowded behind the first, two younger and
somewhat more presentable, the other older, unshaven,
his eyes bloodshot. One of the young ones guffawed.
'Cops getting prettier every day, eh, Jake?'

'Shove it,' the other young one growled. 'Aren't you gonna ask the lady in, Stan?'

Black-bearded Stan said churlishly, 'You wanna come in?'

'No, that's all right, thanks,' Jenny replied, not much liking the looks of Stan or any of his cohorts. 'If you could just tell me which way to go.'

'Trout Brook's that way.' He pointed to the right. 'A mile or so.'

'If you blink, you'll miss it,' Jake supplied. 'Who you lookin' for?'

'A log cabin on the far side of the brook.'

'Only one log place up there, up on the hill. Take the road to the right across the bridge and bear to your right.'

So the cabin existed; Jenny had been beginning to wonder. She gave all four of them a generous smile. 'Thank you. I'm sorry to have disturbed you.'

Stan gave her an inimical look, and before the others could say anything further, closed the door in her face. Jenny turned tail and fled, her boots sucking in the mud as she crossed the end of the driveway. Only a mile to go.

She drove away from the shack, knowing she had interrupted some kind of illegal activity, which, judging by the reek of liquor that had emanated from the four men, could have been bootlegging. They probably had a still back in the woods. What else would there be to do in Trout Brook in the long winter evenings?

The road seemed to be following every loop in the brook, which churned between its banks on her right; to her left the vertical stone face of the mountain launched itself up into the blackness. Miniature avalanches had occurred with disconcerting frequency, leaving tumbled heaps of rocks part way across the road. So Jenny was driving slowly when a black truck with only one headlight careered around the corner and headed straight for her.

She braked and swerved to the right. As the mud grabbed the wheels of her car, jerking it to a halt and throwing her against the steering wheel, the truck passed so close that she saw rust marks in its black paint and braced herself for the scream of metal against metal, the thud of impact. But the truck whipped past with only inches to spare. She heard the diminishing roar of its motor, turned her head and saw the tail lights vanish round the bend. She said a very rude word that was not normally a part of her vocabulary and let out her pent-up breath in a long sigh. Her heart was thumping and her hands shaking so badly that several minutes passed before she opened the door and walked around to the far side of the car to assess the damage.

The two rear hub caps were at least a foot deep in red, glutinous mud. Without much hope of success Jenny got back in the car and tried both reverse and first gear. The car settled a little more deeply in the mud. A tow truck was called for, she knew, but she was willing to bet that Trout Brook would not boast as one of its amenities a garage, let alone a tow truck. Cursing the driver of the black truck, she took her bag and shoes out of the car, locked it, and started walking.

Her raincoat was fashionable rather than waterproof and she had no hat; her hairstyle was ruined almost immediately. She gave thanks for the rubber boots and walked on. Two more turns in the road brought her to a white-painted bridge that crossed the brook, and a road that wound up the hill on the other side to a brightly lit dwelling that might or might not be a log cabin.

As she started across the bridge she felt water trickle down her neck and knew that her raincoat was plastered to her: front, back and sleeves. The legs of her jumpsuit clung to her flesh. So much for sophistication, she thought with a vestige of humour. The green velvet dress would surely have been accompanied by a cloak with an ermine-trimmed hood and dashing leather boots, not to mention a fiery steed and a black-haired hero whose strong arms would have sheltered her from the storm . . .

Because she was too wet to get any wetter, Jenny stopped for a minute and drew a long breath, gazing upwards into the impenetrable black sky from which raindrops swooped to pelt her lips and tongue. The air smelled of wet grass and fallen leaves and dank evergreens, a pungent combination that took her back many years to when she was a little girl riding on her father's tractor in the wood-lot behind the farm. Jenny, you're delaying the inevitable, her inner self chided. Unless you want to spend the night in the car, you have to knock on the door of the log cabin. For she was close enough now to see the rounded, honey-coloured logs that were neatly dovetailed at the corners, and to recognise the BMW parked beside the door. No thanks to Helen's map, she had reached her destination. Phase one was just about complete. The mere thought of phase two filled her with panic.

She drew another slow, steadying breath, thrust her hands into her pockets and walked the last few feet as quickly as she could. Standing in the glow of the outdoor light, she tapped on the door. She heard footsteps, then the door was wrenched open. For a horrible moment she thought black-haired Stan would be standing there, belly straining at his shirt. But the man who opened the door was tall and rangy, with deep blue eyes and thick, dark hair. She said weakly, 'Hello, Graham.'

He grabbed her by the sleeve and hauled her bodily over the step. 'Jenny! Oh my God, *Jenny*! Where the *hell* have you been? I've been out of my mind . . . will you marry me? For God's sake say you'll marry me!'

She gazed up at him, her face blank with shock. 'You were expecting me?'

'Of course I was! I've been tearing my bloody hair out by the roots for the last two hours! Where the devil's your car?'

'I can see where Jason gets his language,' she

muttered, shoving her hands back in her pockets. 'How did you know I was coming?'

'Helen phoned and told me. Said you'd be getting away a little after six. Jenny darling, are you all right?'

'Oh, yes, I'm fine. Graham, what did you say when I walked in the door?'

He finally produced a smile. 'You didn't walk in—I dragged you in. I asked you to marry me.'

'That's what I thought.'

'Well, will you?' There was a sudden, desperate intensity in his face. 'Please say yes, Jenny. I love you so much.'

'I'm not dreaming? This is real?'

Very gently he pinched her cheek. 'No dream.'

Joy and mischief danced in her eyes. 'You're not asking me to marry you just because you want a mother for your children?'

'I'd be the last person to do that.'

'I've walked through rain and wind and driven up and down mountains and talked to bootleggers and put my car in the ditch all to prove to you that I love you for yourself. Because the children aren't here, are they, Graham? You're alone. And it's you I came to see.'

'Car in the ditch?' he repeated sharply.

'Mmm. Up to the axles in lovely red mud.'

'You're not hurt?'

She took a strand of wet hair between her fingers and looked at it with slightly crossed eyes. 'A little damp but not hurt.'

He chuckled. 'Jenny, you can always make me laugh—maybe that's one of the things I love best about you. I'm truly impressed that you've come all the way to Trout Brook to see me—in fact, in a minute or two I'll show you how impressed I am. But you haven't answered the question yet.'

'Yes,' she said.

'You *will* marry me?'

'Yes.'

'Thank God!' he said fervently, and took her in his arms. By the time he had finished kissing her to his satisfaction, the front of his shirt was wet through where it had been pressed against her raincoat. He held her away from him, the pulse throbbing at the base of his throat, and said with a reckless laugh, 'You were understating the case when you said you were a little damp.'

'After that kiss I'm surprised I'm not steaming! Do log cabins come with mirrors?'

'There's one in the bathroom.'

She bent and tugged off her boots, getting mud on her fingers. Then she lined the boots up on the rubber tray by the door and said, 'Lead the way.'

Graham took her by the hand. The front door of the cabin led directly into a single large room, which was a combination of living room, dining room and kitchen, and which boasted a pebblestone fireplace and comfortable furniture in mellow, autumn tones. The bathroom was unashamedly modern. Jenny took off her raincoat, passed it to Graham and looked at herself in the mirror. The jumpsuit was clammily moulded to her skin, the neckline exposing gooseflesh rather than cleavage. Her hair drooped around her ears like hanks of wet rope. Her mascara had run. She struck an attitude and declaimed, 'You see before you the suave, sophisticated Miss Jennifer Sprague, whose plan was to seduce you with her glamour, her elegance and her beauty ... I wouldn't blame you if you ran the other way.'

Negligently he leaned against the wall. 'Nowhere to run to in Trout Brook. Particularly on a night like this. So seduction was on your mind, was it, Miss Jennifer Sprague?'

'I spent at least half an hour before I left fussing with my make-up and my hair,' she complained.

'I have never considered waterproof mascara a prerequisite for seduction.

She smiled at him in the mirror. 'Oh? And what do

you consider the prerequisites, Professor Tyson?'

'A woman who can be soaked to the skin and still set my heart beating as if I were a teenage boy . . . a woman with laughter in her eyes, and generosity in her smile, and love in her heart . . .' His eyes met hers steadily in the mirror. 'A woman of character and intelligence, whose body I ache to possess and whose soul I would share.'

Jenny made a tiny, helpless gesture, her eyes full of tears. 'Oh, Graham . . .'

'I love you, Jenny.'

She turned, wanting to see the man rather than the reflection. 'I love you, too,' she said in a low voice.

'If you start to cry,' he murmured, 'your mascara will really be done for.'

'I—I'd better wash my face.'

'I think you should come into the bedroom and take off those wet clothes. I wouldn't want you to catch pneumonia.'

The moment of choice . . . Jenny walked over to him and touched his damp shirt. 'You could be in danger, too.'

'True.' With a strength that took her breath away, Graham threw his arms around her and held her close. 'Jenny, come and make love to me—so I know you're real. Because maybe, like you, I'm afraid all this is a dream.'

She remembered Mona, who had pushed him away once he had given her a child. She took his hand in hers and said softly, 'Then let us show each other that we are real.'

The bedroom was dimly lit, and cool. Jenny shivered, her mind seizing on details in the room because she was nervous. A sheepskin rug lay on the polished pine floor, which had the same patina as the log walls. The bedspread and curtains were teal-blue; the bed seemed very large.

'You do want to be here, Jenny?'

He was standing a couple of feet away from her, his hands at his sides. He was, when he chose to be, too guarded a man to show his emotions easily; she wondered if he, like herself, was at some level afraid of the transition to intimacy. Certainly he would force nothing on her that she did not wholeheartedly want.

She smiled at him with perfect naturalness. 'I'm cold,' she said. 'I want to be in bed . . . would you mind getting me a towel from the bathroom, Graham?'

As he left the room, she tugged off her sash and jumpsuit, dropping them on the floor. Then she quickly pulled the pins from her hair. She was sitting on the edge of the bed in her lacy black underwear when he came back in. Again her smile was wonderfully natural. 'Thanks—be a dear and dry my hair a bit, will you? I'll soak the pillow like this.' And she tipped her head forward, closing her eyes.

He was gentle with her, his fingers massaging her scalp as the towel drew the rainwater from her hair and fluffed it around her head. Then the towel joined her clothes on the floor. Jenny ran her fingers through her hair, saw the emotion smouldering in his face and knew with a thrill of excitement that he had not been oblivious to the black lace.

She stood up, and as if they had been married for years, starting unbuttoning his shirt. She pulled it free of his waistband, her palms smoothing his skin. Then her fingers reached for the catch on his jeans. 'Help me,' she whispered.

Like a man in a dream he discarded his clothes. But only when she guided his hands to her breast did his control break. He sobbed out her name. Then they fell back on the bed and his hands were everywhere and his kiss opened the floodgates of their mutual need. The scraps of black lace joined the rest of her clothes. With elemental passion her body arched to receive him.

There was little subtlety to that first lovemaking: the subtlety came later, when they woke in the middle of the night to find themselves entwined, and made slow, languorous love in the dark. But the first time was quick and urgent, a blinding voyage of discovery, a desperate search for release.

His tongue brushed her nipple. She moaned with pleasure and saw a fierce, matching pleasure in his face. Then, as if he could not wait, his hand slid down her belly to caress the moist joining of her thighs. Her voice, almost unrecognisable, cried out his name. With sudden confidence, a sureness of touch, his fingers stroked and probed her hot, curving flesh until she trembled and shook and begged him to enter her. Resting his weight on his hands, he obeyed her, agony and delight mingling in the blue, blue eyes. At the first thrust her body convulsed. Inexorably the inward rhythms claimed her, displacing everything but their own imperative, driving her relentlessly towards the explosion of release whose core was, mysteriously, unity. And in the white heat of climax Graham helped her, matched her, joined her, and lost himself in her . . .

Afterwards they lay in each other's arms in awestruck silence. He was still within her. Jenny lay quiet, wishing he could stay for ever, linked to her and held by her, claiming her as his own.

Graham spoke first, his voice overriding the thrum of rain on the roof and the lonely cry of the wind. 'Jenny, that was wonderful. You're wonderful. I feel wonderful.' He gave an exultant laugh. 'You wanted me, didn't you, and you made no secret of it. You gave everything that was yours to give. No holding back. No games, no bargaining . . . I've never experienced such generosity as yours, I want you to know that.'

'Because I love you,' she said simply. 'How could I be other than generous?'

'I don't think you could be . . . because it's your nature to be generous.' His words slowed. 'That's what I began to understand while I was waiting for you—two hours gave me a lot of time to think. You love the children,

Jenny, I know that. I thought somehow that meant you would love me the less . . . but it doesn't mean that at all, doesn't it? Because you're who you are, you have love enough and to spare for all of us.'

'I love *you*, Graham.' Her voice shook with the strength of her feelings.

'Sweetheart . . .' He kissed her, to their mutual and entire satisfaction.

'I'd love you if you didn't have any children at all,' Jenny announced, knowing how important it was that she say those words.

His kiss reassured her that he believed her, loved her, and might quite easily be enticed into demonstrating that love. *'Again?'* she murmured. 'So soon?'

'Again and again. For as long as we live,' he said fiercely.

She held him close. 'I didn't know I could be this happy.'

'I hope I can always make you happy, Jenny. Which brings me to something else I want to say. I love my children. But I don't want our marriage to be overwhelmed by children and domesticity. We'll take illicit weekends away from them, and holidays with just the two of us.'

With lazy sensuality she ran her fingers down his spine. 'Any kind of a weekend with you sounds like heaven.'

'I can't concentrate when you do that.'

'Complaining?'

He laughed. 'Do you think we'll still fight, Jenny?'

'I expect so. Sometimes. But they'll be good, honest fights.'

He grabbed her wandering hand, imprisoning it against his chest. 'Be serious, woman. Because there's something else I want to tell you . . . Do you know how I visualise our marriage, our whole relationship? As the certainty that no matter what happens in the world out there, no matter what people say or do to you all day,

there is the one sure place where you can be accepted for
yourself and let down all the barriers, knowing you're
safe ... I never had that certainty with Mona. But I
have it with you.'

'Nor did I with Marc,' Jenny said slowly, knowing
her words for the truth. Although when Marc had
broken their engagement she had been shocked, she had
recognised afterwards that there had been warning
signals she had ignored: that the ripe curves of her body
had mocked him with the knowledge that she could not
bear his child.

'I've only made love to you once, Jenny, but I feel
closer to you, more truly intimate with you than I've felt
with anyone else in my life.'

He was echoing her feelings exactly. She snuggled a
little closer, if that were possible, and suddenly
remembered something she had pushed aside when
Graham had so precipitately proposed to her in the
doorway of the cabin. 'Graham, you said Helen phoned
to tell you I was coming, didn't you? Did she really say I
was leaving at six?'

He nuzzled her neck. 'Mmm.'

'I told her I'd be leaving at eight.'

She had his attention now. 'Two hours later?'

'I'm sure that's what I told her.'

'She knew I'd worry about you on a night like this,'
Graham said grimly. 'It was while I was waiting that I
came to my senses and realised that the children had
nothing to do with how I felt about you ... what's the
betting Helen did that on purpose?'

'Fairly high, I would think. I wouldn't be surprised if
she even left out a couple of crucial turns on the map to
be sure I wouldn't get here too fast ... you've got quite a
sister, Graham.'

'To her credit, I'm sure she caught on that I was in
love with you. Helen's never been known for her
patience, she probably wanted to speed things up a bit.'

Lazily Jenny tickled his ribs. 'I'm glad she did . . . aren't you?'

'You could say so.'

'She's bringing the children out tomorrow. Phase three of her plan to get you and me together.' Briefly Jenny described Helen's strategy. 'So they're arriving about eleven to convince you to make an honest woman out of me.'

'Overkill.'

She stretched sinuously as his hand caressed her hip. 'Do that again . . . oh Graham, I'm so happy!'

'So you like phase two. So do I. It could last a long time—like the rest of our lives.'

They fell asleep to the sound of the rain. They woke and made love and slept again. And the next time Jenny woke her watch said ten-fifteen. She stared at it in disbelief, put it to her ear, heard its ticking, and grabbed Graham's bare shoulder. 'Wake up! The children could be here in half an hour.'

He opened his eyes, yawned lazily and pulled her down on top of him. 'Giving me orders already?'

She tried to wriggle free. 'Graham, they mustn't find us in bed!'

'Then you'd better hold still. Because when you move your breasts like that, I don't feel like getting out of bed.'

She blushed. 'I'm not trying to be seductive!'

'You don't have to try, my sweet. Particularly in your present unclothed state. Kiss me.'

'My jumpsuit's still wet—what will I *wear*?'

'Don't panic, there's a drier. Didn't you hear what I said?'

'I did. But one kiss is just as likely to lead to a second, and then a third.' She let her hand wander down his body. 'And so on.'

His laugh was as spontaneous as a young boy's. 'How well you know me! What time are the children leaving Brockton? Not that they need to come at all. I did propose to you, didn't I, when you arrived last night?'

'You did. And I accepted.' She moved her hand again. 'Unless you want to change your mind?'

'I have no intention of changing my mind. But maybe we should let the children have their say.' He ran his hands up and down her back. 'Come on, Jenny, get out of bed.'

'But I don't want to now,' she murmured, nibbling his ear. 'How's that for inconsistency?'

'We'd better get married soon, so we can go to bed legitimately.'

She kissed him. 'Whenever you say.'

'Did I ever tell you I loved you, Jennifer Sprague?'

When Jenny caught sight of her watch-face again, it said ten forty-five. She scrambled out of bed, had a shower while her jumpsuit was drying, bundled her hair into a knot on top of her head, and tried to wipe the idiotic grin off her face. The children would not understand the blue shadows under her eyes, but Helen would.

Jenny and Graham were sitting respectably in the living room drinking coffee when a vehicle came up the driveway. Graham went to open the door. He kissed Helen, took Jason from her arms and smiled at the other two children. 'Hello, you guys. Nice to see you. Helen, I gather you and Jenny have already met?'

Helen looked elegant and at ease in tailored pants and a matching jacket. 'We have indeed.' She winked at Jenny. 'I can tell that phase two proceeded according to plan.'

Her brother said lightly, 'Several times.'

'You know about it?' Helen asked, losing a little of her poise.

'I not only know about it, I thoroughly enjoyed its implementation.'

'Really, Graham . . . the children have something to say to you.'

The two older children were still grouped by the door. *Two against the world*, thought Jenny with an inward chuckle. They looked very solemn; neither of them had as yet spoken a word. Because she knew what was coming, and because she knew she was going to live with them and become part of their lives, she felt an overwhelming surge of love for them.

Daniel said portentously, 'We're a deputation.'

'I see,' said Graham with equal seriousness, sitting down and putting Jason on the floor.

'We got an—an affidavit,' Daniel pronounced, pulling a piece of paper from the back pocket of his jeans and unfolding it. 'I wrote it and we both signed it. You gotta be quiet, Jason, while we read it.'

Jason smiled angelically at Jenny. 'Dadada,' he said. She picked him up and hugged him. 'Hush for a minute.'

'Okay,' said Daniel, clearing his throat and beginning to read. 'We, the undersigned—Aunt Helen told us that bit—want Dad, otherwise known as Graham Michael Tyson, to marry Jenny, otherwise known as Jennifer Sprague.' He grinned engagingly at Jenny. 'We didn't know your middle name.'

'Margaret,' she said.

'Jennifer Margaret Sprague. I wanted to say spinster of this parish 'cause that's what the minister says in church when they read out the banns, but Gillie wouldn't let me.'

'Spinster sounds like a little old lady with grey hair,' Gillie said stubbornly. 'Jenny's not like that.'

Daniel frowned at the paper. 'The reasons are as follows:

(1) We like Mrs Layton okay but she's not like a real mother.

(2) We want a real mother.

(3) We all like Jenny, specially after Snowflake's funeral, and we think she'd make a good mother.

(4) So we think Dad, otherwise known as Graham

Michael Tyson, should ask Jenny to marry him.
Signed: Daniel Tyson
Gillie Tyson.'

He held the paper out to his father. 'We got Jason to make an X at the bottom, 'cause we know he likes Jenny, too.'

Graham took the paper, his face straight, and read it through. 'Very cogent arguments,' he said, and got to his feet. He looked at Jenny, all his love in his eyes. 'Miss Jennifer Margaret Sprague, spinster of the parish of Brockton, may I request the honour of your hand in marriage?'

From the corner of her eye Jenny saw the two children gape at their father; they had presumably expected an argument, or perhaps even a flat refusal. With equal ceremony, holding Jason to her breast, she stood up and said, 'I accept your proposal, Dr Tyson. With pleasure.'

'Four witnesses,' he said. 'You can't get out of it now, Jenny.'

'I don't want to.'

'So we are officially betrothed and the wedding will take place at the earliest possible date.'

'Betrothed?' said Daniel.

'Engaged. Affianced. Plighted. She'll marry me, Daniel.'

Gillie's face was ecstatic. 'You really will, Jenny?'

'Yes.'

'That was easy,' Daniel said, looking a little disappointed, 'We figured we'd have to fight.'

'You're supposed to kiss her, Dad,' Gillie ordered with a bounce of impatience. 'To show that you love her. You do, don't you?'

'More than I can say, Gillie.' He leaned over, Jason's eyes following every move, and gave Jenny a chaste kiss on the mouth.

'Now what?' said Daniel, the practical, with an eight-year-old's scorn for romance.

Helen, who had watched the whole proceeding with a satisfied smile, said, 'I just happen to have a bottle of champagne in the car, as well as some ginger ale. A celebration is called for.'

'A party!' Gillie crowed.

'I don't like champagne,' Daniel said, very much a man of the world.

'How do you know?' Graham demanded.

'I tasted it at Mr Garvey's wedding last year. It gets up your nose and makes you sneeze.'

'There are those who would not agree with you, Daniel, but at your age I'm just as glad that champagne is not your favourite drink.' He sat down on the chesterfield, pulling Jenny down beside him, and the children crowded round. 'You know what we have to do first of all? We have to teach Jason to call Jenny Mama instead of Dada.'

'Good luck,' Jenny remarked.

As Helen came back in with a picnic hamper, Daniel said distrustfully, 'Did you know all along that Dad was going to say yes, Aunt Helen?'

'I had my suspicions. Better to be safe than sorry. I even brought a chocolate cake—just in case.'

Graham popped the cork from the champagne bottle while Helen cut the cake in generous slices and poured the ginger ale. The champagne had to be drunk from water tumblers. Helen raised her glass. 'I propose a toast,' she said. 'To Jenny and Graham, many years of happiness.'

Graham smiled at Jenny. 'An ideal match.'

Jason dug his fingers into the chocolate icing and also smiled at her. 'Dadada,' he said.

Harlequin Presents

Coming Next Month

Available in June wherever paperback books are sold, or through Harlequin Reader Service:

In the U.S.
901 Fuhrmann Blvd.
P.O. Box 1397
Buffalo, N.Y. 14240-1397

In Canada
P.O. Box 603
Fort Erie, Ontario
L2A 5X3

Take 4 books
& a surprise gift
FREE

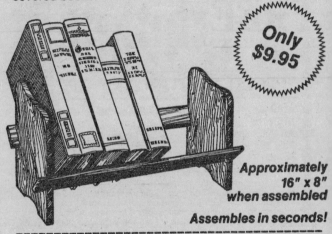

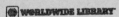

Hannah, and as soon as the door closed behind them, Chad covered his face with his hands. 'My God!' he groaned, 'I've just had the most sobering thought!'

'What?' she asked, alarmed.

'Hugo! It's just occurred to me. When we're married, he'll be my *brother-in-law*!'

'Oh, you poor *thing*!' she squealed, her shoulders shaking with laughter. 'And Melissa—she'll be your *sister-in-law*!'

Chad reached for her and pulled her down on the sofa, his mouth nuzzling her neck, her shoulders, her earlobes, finally resting on the dimple by her mouth. 'What a lucky man I am,' he told her happily, 'to have all three of you!'

Andrea reached up to touch his cheek, her fingers trailing lightly across his mouth. 'When Hugo went fishing in your pond that day, it was you he was fishing for all along.'

'And I fell for it,' Chad grinned, 'hook, line and sinker!'

'I don't even think he had any bait that day, either,' Andrea teased.

'Sure he did,' Chad corrected her. 'He had his beautiful sister. A girl called Andy!'

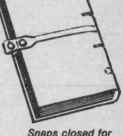